Days of Dust

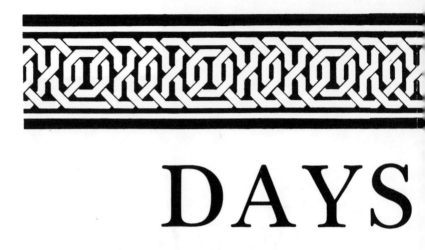

DAYS

Translated by Trevor Le Gassick
Introduction   Edward Said

# of DUST

Halim Barakat

Three Continents Press
1346 Connecticut Avenue, N.W.
Washington, D.C.

© Halim Barakat 1983

First Edition in this format by
Three Continents Press
1346 Connecticut Avenue N.W.
Washington, D.C. 20036

Second printing 1986

'Awdat al-Ta'ir ila-l-Bahr *is the original Arabic title of this novel which appeared in
1969 published by Dar al-Nahar, Beirut, Lebanon.*

This English translation by Trevor Le Gassick under the title Days of Dust *first
appeared in 1974 published by Medina University Press,
Wilmette, Illinois.*

A French translation of this novel by Claude Krul under the title Le Vaisseau
Reprend le Large *appeared in 1979 published by Editions
Naaman, Quebec, Canada.*

A Japanese translation of this novel by Seiji Takai and Kenji Sekine under the title
Umi Ni Kaeru Toki *appeared in 1980 published by Kawade
Shobo Shinsha, Tokyo, Japan.*

Cover Design by Kamal Boullata
Photo of Halim Barakat by Richard Cassis

ISBN: 0-89410-359-8
ISBN: 0-89410-360-1 (pbk)
LC No: 82-74265

3CP

CONTENTS

INTRODUCTION *Edward Said*   ix

TRANSLATOR'S FOREWORD *Trevor Le Gassick*   xxxv

PART ONE   1
  The Threshold
  June 11–June 20, 1967

PART TWO   11
  Voices Surge and the South Wind Rages
  June 5–June 10, 1967
    The First Day: Thunder in the Voices of Children, 13
    The Second Day: The Sailor Returns to the Sea, 41
    The Third Day: Death Is a Field, 79
    The Fourth Day: Jacob Circumcises the Palestinians, 103
    The Fifth Day: Death Shall Have No Dominion, 123
    *The Sixth Day: Floods in the Streets and Ants Creeping
      through the Arteries of the Heart, 143*

PART THREE   161
  Numerous Days of Dust
  June 11–June 20, 1967

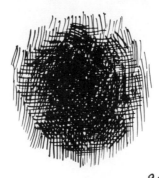

وَرَأَى العربيُّ كُلَّ ما فعلاه فَإِذَا هُوَ سَيِّئٌ جِدًّا

Where storm and raging wind
   impel me,
Over the wat'ry waste I roam;
How long tis? Hardly can I tell
   thee,
I mark no more of years the sum!
I cannot name, shouldst thou
   demand it,
The many seas I've wandered o'er:
The only aim my heart doth long
   for,
Ne'er shall I reach,—my native
   shore!

To the land drives the storm.
Sails are in!
Anchor down!
To the bay hurry in!
Swarthy Captain, go on land,
Now that sev'n long years have
   flown!
Seek a faithful maiden's hand!
Faithful maiden, be his own!
Winds be thy wedding-song,
Ocean is dancing, too!
Hark! he pipes! What!
Captain, hast thou return'd?
Set the sails!
And thy bride—say, where is she?
Off to sea!
As of old, as of old,
No good fortune for thee!
Blow, thou stormwind, howl and
   blow!
What care we how fast we go!
We have sails from Satan's store,—
Sails that last for evermore!

INTRODUCTION

Edward Said

READING IS INEVITABLY a complex, comparative process. A novel in particular, if it is not to be read reductively as an item of sociopolitical evidence, involves the reader with itself not only because of its writer's skill but also because of other novels. All novels belong to a family, and any reader of novels is a reader of this complex family to which they all belong. *How* they belong, however, is a very difficult problem to settle in cases where the novel in question is not in the central Western European or American tradition. In that tradition there is a recognizable genealogy, going as far back as *The Odyssey* and *Don Quixote,* but concentrated primarily in the eighteenth, nineteenth, and the main part of the twentieth centuries. What we have become accustomed to is the novel as a line to which non-European or non-American novels in the modern period offer puzzling alternatives. Are these novels "imitations" (which, minus the euphemism, means colonial copies of "the great tradition")? Are they original works in their own right? Are they neither?

Such alternatives, I think, confuse us more than they help us to read with understanding. Comparing novels of equal merit but from different traditions cannot mean, and never has meant, judging one over the other as more original or more of a copy. All literature, in a certain narrow mimetic sense, is a "copy" of something; originality is really the art of recombining the familiar. And this is precisely the premise upon which the novel is based. Not only do novels "imitate" reality, but they also imitate each other: this is the natural condition of their existence and the secret of their persistence as a form. But if the Western European novel has a long linear genealogy linking its members to each other (in ways we shall presently examine), in the more recent novelistic traditions, of which the Arabic is one, both the history and the structure of the form are different. The difference is primarily a matter of the form's existence (shorter in the Arabic novel, which effectively begins in this century), of the circumstances of history, and of the aesthetic method.

In a short introduction of this kind one can scarcely begin to take in all these differences; nor, for that matter, can one expect to treat the Arabic novel with the detail or care it requires. But I shall try to suggest first how the Arabic novel in its history and development redistributes, or disperses, the conditions under which the Western European novel has existed. This will take up the opening part of my discussion, after which I shall describe the exigencies of contemporary Arabic prose, particularly those operating after 1948. I hope thus to provide the reader of the present translation with some historical and aesthetical service when he compares, as he must, Arabic writing with other sorts.

In the two and a half centuries of its existence the Western European novel has been the creation of both a particular historical development and the rise, then the triumph, of the middle class. Not less an institution for all the intricacies of its method, the variety of its subject matter, the powerful entrancement of its psychological and aesthetical structures, and the sheer detail of its vision, the novel is the most time-bound and circumstantial as well as the most universal of all postclassical literary forms. Yet history *in* the novel and history *of* the novel—what the novel in Stendhal's image reflects of life as in a mirror and what the novel's own internal history as a form of literature is—these are very different things.[1] The first, I think, is a constant pressure: every novelist is of his time, however much his imagination may take him beyond it. Each novelist articulates a consciousness of his time that he shares with the group of which historical circumstances (class, period, perspective) make him a part. Thus even in its irreducible singularity the novelistic work *is itself* a historical reality—one whose articulation is doubtless more fine, more circumstanced and idiomatic with regard to its moment, than other human experiences. Narrative, in short, is the historical mode as it is most traditionally understood. But what makes it possible to distinguish Marx's *The Class Struggles in France* from Flaubert's *L'Education sentimentale*—both works whose subject is the 1848 revolution—is the history of the type of narrative incorporated within the narrative. Marx's belongs eccentrically to a tradition of analysis and polemic taken in part from journalism; Flaubert's, no less eccentric in its own way, no less polemic, stands squarely within an institutional tradition, the novel's, whose language, pressures, and audience Flaubert assumes—and puts to work on his behalf—as Marx cannot assume for his work.

Between the middle of the eighteenth century and, roughly, the first third of this century, to write a novel meant that it was impossible for the novelist to ignore the history and tradition of the form. I put the statement in this negative way in order to emphasize the extraordinarily fertile polarity existing within each good novel: the polarity between the claims of the novel's internal history and those of the novelist's individual imagination.

In no small measure to write a novel was, for Dickens, Eliot, Flaubert, Balzac, to have received and further sustained the institution of prose fiction. Just as their subject matter is frequently a variation on the family romance, with a hero or heroine attempting to create his or her own destiny against the bonds of family, so too the great classical novels of the nineteenth century are themselves a massive aesthetic dynasty to which even the most powerful imaginations are necessarily apprentices or children. The relation of Tolstoy to Stendhal, or of Dostoevski to Balzac and Dickens, exactly illustrates the manner in which even the most original imaginations considered themselves heirs of an aesthetic past that they were extending into their own times. Thus each novel imitates not only reality but also every other novel. It was *because of* his imagination that Tolstoy could benefit from, by imitating, the novel's own history as represented to him by Stendhal; for the particular marvel of prose fiction was its power to employ creatively its own genealogy over and over. This is especially true of every great novel, whose novelty was (perhaps surprisingly) in making the transmitted institutions of prose fiction serve as a defense against the unmediated urgency either of individual imagination or of the historical moment. Since, as Lukács has said, "the novel is the epic of a world that has been abandoned by God," then "the mental attitude of the novel is virile maturity, and the characteristic structure of its matter is discreteness, the separation between interiority and adventure."[2] The novel's secular world is maintained by an author whose maturity depends on distinctions, inherited from the novel's history, between pure subjective fantasy and pure factual chronicle, between directionless brooding and an unlimited episodic repetition.

In all these ways, then, time—or rather temporality grasped in the complex ways I have been discussing—is the novel's life: as historical moment and as history of the form, temporality makes the world's pressure amenable to verbal structure. Yet such a life in Western Europe and, to a certain extent, in nineteenth-century America has enjoyed the broad support of readers and critics. They too contribute to the novel as an institution. From Fielding's digressive essays on the novel in his novels, through Sterne's technical brilliance, through Stendhal's and Balzac's critical work, and on into the commentary and metacommentary of such writers as Proust, Henry James, and James Joyce, the novel has employed novelists as critics. Moreover it has produced critics both professional and amateur—one remembers Dickens' avid periodical subscribers who always knew what it was they wanted from the novelist—sustaining the discipline, and the reality, of the form. This interplay between reader and writer has been unique in prose fiction: it has its origin perhaps in Part Two of Cervantes' *Don Quixote,* where the errant protagonist encounters men and women who have read Part One and expect—indeed, dictate—certain actions from him. In one sense readers of fiction through the years of its maturity have played almost as great a role in the form's flourishing as have the writers.

A dramatically different situation obtains in the history of the modern Arabic novel. The twentieth-century novel in Arabic has a variety of forebears, none of them formally and dynastically prior and useful as, say, in the rather directly useful way that Fielding antedates Dickens. Arabic literature before the twentieth century has a rich assortment of narrative forms—*qissa, sira, hadith, khurafa, ustura, khabar, nadira, magama*—of which no one seems to have become, as the European novel did, the major narrative type. The reasons for this are extremely complex, and they cannot occupy us here (elsewhere I have speculated on one reason for this difference between Arabic-Islamic and European prose fiction: whereas the former literary tradition views reality as plentiful, complete, and divinely directed, the latter sees reality as radically incomplete, authorizing innovation, and problematic).[3] The fact remains, however, that there is a modern Arabic novel which, during the twentieth century, has undergone numerous and interesting transformations. Today it has produced a very wide variety of talents, styles, critics, readers, all mostly unknown or deliberately ignored outside the Middle East; surely the ruling Western obsession with Arabs exclusively (or nearly so) as a political problem is largely to blame for this lamentable failure in knowledge. There is less of an excuse for this failure today, as Trevor Le Gassick's sensitive translations (e.g., of Naguib Mahfouz' *Midaq Alley,* Halim Barakat's *Days of Dust*) begin to gain the currency they surely deserve.[4]

Yet the peculiarly fascinating background of issues formal and issues historical and psychological faced by the contemporary Arabic novelist needs some elucidation, particularly if one takes the period after 1948, and that after 1967, as shaping an intelligible historical period for the novelistic imagination. Particularly also if this period is considered as constitutive of the common subject matter presented to any and all writers in the Arab East, not simply novelists, during the past quarter century. Even more particularly if the course of the European novel is kept in mind as a *comparative fact* with which the Arabic novel *produces* valuable differences. I shall try to present this period, then, with its two great demarcations in 1948 and 1967, from the point of view of any Arab wishing to write. Allowing for a modicum of opportunism and bad writing during the years since 1948, I believe that Arabs who wrote (novels, plays, poetry, history, philosophy, political polemic, etc.) undertook a fundamentally heroic enterprise, a project of self-definition and autodidactic struggle unexampled on such a scale since World War II. Consider first the setting that offered itself as historical moment. After decades of internal struggle against political chaos and foreign domination, a struggle in which politico-national identity was still at its most precarious initial stage—with religion, demography, modernity, language enmeshed confusingly with each other—Arabs everywhere were forced additionally to confront as their own problem, taking an especially provocative form, one of the greatest and still unsolved problems of Western civilization, the Jewish question. To say that 1948 made an extraordinary cultural and historical demand on the Arab is to be guilty of the crassest understatement. The year and the processes which it culminated represent an explosion whose effects continue to fall unrelentingly into the present. No Arab, however armed he was at those and later moments by regional or tribal or religious nationalism, could ignore the event. Not only did 1948 put forth unprecedented challenges to a collectivity already undergoing the political evolution of several European centuries compressed into a few decades: this after all was mainly a difference of detail between the Arab East and all other Third World countries, since the end of colonialism meant the beginning and the travail of uncertain national selfhood. But 1948 put forward a monumental enigma, an existential mutation for which Arab history was unprepared.

An Egyptian might say that the events of 1948 pressed on the Palestinian Arab the most closely; so too might an Iraqi, a Lebanese, a Sudanese. Yet no Arab could say that in 1948 he was in any serious way detached or apart from the events in Palestine. He might reasonably say that he was shielded from Palestine; but he could not say—because his language and his religious, cultural tradition implicated him at every turn—that he was any less a loser, an Arab, as a result of what happened in Palestine. Furthermore nothing in his history, that is, in the repertory or vocabulary provided to him by his historical experience, gave him an adequate method for representing the Palestine drama to himself. Arab nationalism, Islamic traditionalism, regional creeds, small-scale communal or village solidarities—all these stopped short of the general result of Zionist success and the particular experience of Arab defeat. No concept seemed large enough, no language precise enough to take in the common fate. What happened could not be put down to a flaw in the Arab character (since no such character was ever articulated), nor to a divine decree against the faithful, nor to a trivial accident in a faraway place.

The magnitude of such events is indicated, I think, in one of the words most usually employed to describe them, the Arabic word *nakba*. Its most celebrated use is in the title of Constantine Zurayk's 1948 book, *Ma'na al-nakba* [The meaning of the disaster];[5] yet even in Zurayk's work, which advances an interpretation of the Zionist victory as a challenge to the whole of Arab modernity, another of the meanings of *nakba* is in play. For the word suggests in its root that affliction or disaster is somehow brought about by, and hence linked by necessity to, deviation, a veering out of course, a serious deflection away from a forward path. (This incidentally is in marked contrast to another, less commonly employed word for 1967: *naksa*, which suggests nothing more radical than a relapse, a temporary setback, as in the process of recovery from an illness.) The development of Zurayk's argument in his book led him, as it was to lead many other writers since 1948, to interpret *al-nakba* as a rupture of the most profound sort. It is true that Zionism exposed the Arabs' disunity, lack of technological culture, political unpreparedness, and so on; more significant, however, was the fact that the disaster caused a rift to appear between the Arabs and the very possibility of their historical continuity as a people. So strong was the deflection, or the deviation, from the Arabs' persistence in time up to 1948, that the issue for the Arabs became whether what was "natural" to them—their continued national duration in history—would be possible at all.

There is an interesting paradox here, and it is one that would inform Arab writing thereafter. Zurayk was saying in fact that the deviation was so strong as to put the Arabs, as a people, in historical question. Yet he was also saying that the disaster had revealed to the Arabs that their history had itself not yet made of them a nation. So from the perspective of the past, the Arabs would seem to have swerved from the path toward national identity, union, and so on; from the perspective of the future, the disaster raised the specter of national extinction. The paradox is that both of these observations hold, so that at the intersection of past and future stands the disaster, which on the one hand reveals the deviation from *what has yet to happen* (a unified, collective Arab identity) and on the other reveals the possibility of *what may happen* (Arab extinction as a cultural or national unit). The true force then of Zurayk's book is that it made clear the problem of the *present,* a problematic site of contemporaneity, occupied and blocked from the Arabs. For the Arabs to act knowingly was to *create* the present, and this was a battle of restoring historical continuity, healing a rupture, and—most important—forging a historic possibility.

It is for all these reasons that a very high premium is placed, in Zurayk's argument, upon what he called the creative elite. The elite's role, essentially considered, was to articulate the present in the precise historical and realistic terms which, as we have seen, the disaster threatened with obliteration. To speak or to write in Arabic was to articulate not only the lingua franca but also the reality—the possibility of an Arab contemporaneity—very precariously held within the present. Without referring back to Zurayk's book of 1948, Anwar Abdel Malek, the Egyptian sociologist, powerfully elaborated on the nature, and the language, of struggle. As recently as the seventies, Abdel Malek was arguing that Arab-Islamic civilization, although prey to economic and political imperialism, was most seriously endangered, in the long run, by its susceptibility to cultural imperialism, the principal feature of which was to impose on the Arabs a sort of impediment whose purpose was to prevent direct ties between them and Asia and Africa. Unless Arab culture, employing the full resources of its *specificity* (the word has great urgency for Abdel Malek), could participate freely in its own self-making, it would be as if it did not exist.[6]

In such a context, then, the role of any writer who considered himself seriously engaged in the actuality of his time—and few writers during the period since 1948 considered themselves otherwise engaged—was, first of all, as a producer of thought and language whose radical intention was to guarantee survival to what was in imminent danger of extinction. Beginning with the Egyptian Revolution of 1952, the rise of movements of national liberation provided opportunities for a dialectical vision in which the crises of the present would become the cornerstones of the future. Writing therefore became a historical act and, according to the Egyptian literary critic Ghali Shukry, after 1967, an act of resistance. If before 1948 the Arab novel could be described *sui generis* as a novel of historical recapitulation, then after 1948 it became a novel of historical and social development.[7] This is especially evident in the Egyptian novel. Even though a so-called romantic (i.e., sentimental, backward-looking) alternative existed for writers such as Yusuf el-Siba'i, the large theme of most Egyptian novels after 1948 was, as Shukry observed, the near-tragic conflict between a protagonist and some "outside" force.[8] The imperatives for the writer were to increase the refinement and detail of his portrayals; or, as Ragai al-Naqqash phrased in a polemical letter to Nazik al-Mala'ikah (the Iraqi poetess), writing was not and could not be free: it had to put itself at life's service. This was another way of identifying the writer's role directly with the problematics of Arab contemporaneity.[9]

The Arab writer's role was further aggravated by the internal conflict he experienced between his particular regional identity and his transregional or Arab-Islamic ambition. Yet even in such vastly different assertions of regional identity as Hussayn Fawzi's work on Egyptian civilization, or Said Aql's on Lebanese poetics, or in the ideologies of such movements as the Syrian Nationalist party and the Ba'ath, there remained, always, the web of circumstance that enmeshed every Arab, from Algeria to the Gulf. So strong was it—as I described it above in terms of a paradoxical present—that the primary task seemed always to be one of *making* the present in such a way as, once again, to *make* it in touch with past authenticity and future possibility. The past is usually identified with loss, the future with uncertainty. But as for the present, it is a constant experience, a *scene* to be articulated with all the resources of language and vision. Even when the writer's aim is to render the present as disaster, the more so after the war óf 1967, it is the *scene* as the irreducible form of the present which the writer must affirm.

Here we must remark another complexity. Just as there is no traditional Arab novel, there is no real Arab drama, or at least no long-standing and unbroken dramatic tradition. There are considerable dramatic attainments, however—mostly, as is the case with the novel, of the period after World War I. So here, too, when one speaks of a scene, there is a kind of eccentricity implied, unique to the writer in Arabic. What the dramatic and prose scene have in common, first of all, is the sense of *contested space*. Whether it is a page or the proscenium arch theater, the writer fills it with language struggling to maintain a presence. Such an attitude leads to very definite technical and aesthetic consequences. If the unit of composition is the scene, and not the period (prologue, middle, end, in the Aristotelian sense), then the connection between scenes is tenuous. There is a tendency in fact to episodism, and the repetition of scenes, as if the rhythmic succession of scenes can become a substitute for quasi-organic continuity. It is a striking fact that the principal successes of artistic prose and drama, even from before 1948—for example, Taha Hussayn's *Al-ayyam,* Tawfiq al-Ḥakim's *Yaw-miyat na'ib fil aryaf,* the comedies of Naguib al-Rihani, the films of Kamal Salim and Niyazi Mustapha, the works of Khalil Gibran, Jabra Jabra's novella *Surakh fil layl tawil*—are formally a succession of scenes held together more in the style of a journal than in that of the Aristotelian model. Unlike the journal, however, these works are built out of discretely shaped scenes in which a continuous play of substitutions takes place; entrances and appearances, for instance, play the role of ontological affirmation. Conversely, absences and exits seem to threaten extinction or a quasi death. To be in a scene is to displace extinction, to substitute life for the void. Thus the very act of telling, narrating, uttering, guarantees actuality; here the Islamic tradition of the *isnad* is vitalized and put to a definite aesthetic purpose.

The author's persona is very frequently the *spectator,* engaged enough in what he is telling about to be a character, disengaged enough to be able to point out the abuses, the comedy or melodrama of what is taking place before him in the narration. Tawfiq al-Hakim's persona often speaks of *masrah al-hayat* ("the theater of life"), which is less a figure of speech than an aesthetic method. Each episode is a scene of enactment whose importance is revealed to be not that it took place (all of the scenes are scenes of habitual occurrences) but that it is being recorded and being narrated to someone; in the action of narration and transmission, the habitual is exposed for the often lurid abuse of humanity that it is. Even the abuse itself conforms to the pattern. Once, for example, the narrator is told a story—an episode within an episode—by a doctor who, after being summoned to a poor village patient, discovers her lying on her back with a baby's arm protruding from her womb. He learns from the old midwife that after the fetus' death three days before, she stuffed the woman's womb with straw, and the two of them waited patiently under God's protection (*sitr rabbuna*).[10] Since the woman has died, and since *sitr* means literally to disguise or shelter with a screen or curtain, the entire episode doubles over itself as it sets in motion, through narrative enactment, the interplay of scene, substitution, recurrence, absence, death, and, finally, scene again.

The emphasis on scenes therefore is intensified, is made more urgent, after 1948: a scene formally translates the critical issues at stake in the Arab world. This is not a matter of proving how literature or writing *reflects* life, nor is it confirmation of an allegorical interpretation of Arab reality: for, unfortunately, these approaches to modern Arabic writing are endemic to most of the very scarce Western analyses of the literature.[11] What is of greater interest is how the scene *is itself* the very problem of Arabic literature and writing after the disaster of 1948: the scene does not merely reflect the crisis, or historical duration, or the paradox of the present. Rather, the scene *is contemporaneity* in its most problematic and even rarified form. In no place can one see this more effectively than in prose directly concerned with the events in Palestine. Here is the opening scene of Ghassan Kanafani's novella *Rijal fil shams,* certainly his finest work and one of the subtlest and most powerful of modern novellas.

Abu Qais laid his chest on the dirt wet with dew. Immediately the earth began to throb: a tired heart's beats, flooding through the sand grains, seeping into his very innermost being . . . and every time he threw his chest against the dirt he felt the same palpitation, as if the earth's heart had not stopped since that first time he laid himself down, since he tore a hard road from the deepest hell toward an approaching light, when he once told of it to his neighbor who shared the cultivation of a field with him, there on the land he had left ten years ago. His reply was derision: "What you hear is the sound of your own heart plastered to the earth." What tiresome malice! And the smell, how does he explain that? He inhaled it, as it swam through his brow, then passed fadingly into his veins. Every time he breathed as he lay supine he imagined himself drinking in the smell of his wife's hair as she had stepped out after bathing it in cold water. . . . That haunting fragrance of a woman's hair, washed in cold water and, still damp, spread out to dry, covering her face. . . . The same pulse: as if a small bird was sheltered between your cupped palms. . . .[12]

The scene continues as Abu Qais slowly awakens to a realization of his exact surroundings, somewhere near the estuary of the Tigris and the Euphrates; he is there awaiting arrangements to be made to take him illegally into Kuwait, where he hopes to find work. As in the passage quoted above, he will "understand" his location, and the scene's setting in the present, by way of a recollection out of his past: his teacher's voice, in a Palestinian village schoolhouse, intoning the geography lesson, a description of the estuary. Abu Qais' own present is an amalgam of disjointed memory with the gathering intrusive force of his intolerable situation: he is a refugee, with a family, forced to seek employment in a country whose blinding sun signifies the universal indifference to his fate. We will discover that the approaching light is a proleptic reference to the novella's final episode: along with two other Palestinian refugees, Abu Qais is being smuggled into Kuwait in the empty belly of a tanker-truck. The three of them are left in the truck while the border inspection is being negotiated. Under the sun the three die of suffocation, unable even to give a sign.

This passage is one of the numerous scenes into which the work is divided. In almost every one, the present, temporally speaking, is unstable and seems subject to echoes from the past, to synaesthesia as sight gives way to sound or smell and as one sense interweaves with another, to a combination of defensiveness against the harsh present and the protection of some particularly cherished fragment of the past. Even in Kanafani's style—which seems clumsy in my translation, but I thought it important to render the complex sentence structure as exactly as I could—one is unsure of the points in time to which the center of consciousness (one of the three men) refers. In the passage above, "every time" blends into "since that first time," which also seems to include, obscurely, "there on the land he had left ten years ago." Those three clauses are dominated figuratively by the image of tearing a road out of darkness toward the light. Later, during the main part of the novella, we will remark that much of the action takes place in the dusty street of an Iraqi town where the three men, independent of each other, petition, plead, bargain with "specialists" to take them across the border. The main conflict in the book therefore turns about that contest in the present: impelled by exile and dislocation, the Palestinian must carve a path for himself in existence, which is by no means a "given" or stable reality for him. Like the land he left, his past seems broken off just before it could bring forth fruit; yet the man has family, responsibilities, life itself to answer to, in the present. Not only is his future uncertain; even his present situation increases in difficulty as he barely manages to maintain his balance in the swirling traffic of the dusty street. Day, sun, the present: those are at once there, hostile, and goads to him to move on out of the sometimes misty, sometimes hardened protection of memory and fantasy. When the men finally move out of their spiritual desert into the present, toward the future which they reluctantly but necessarily choose, they will die—invisibly, anonymously, killed in the sun, in the same present that has summoned them out of their past and taunted them with their helplessness and inactivity.

For Kanafani a scene is centrally the convenience given to the writer by the general novelistic tradition; what he uses in order to present the action, therefore, is a device which, displaced from the tradition that can take it for granted, ironically comments on the rudimentary struggles facing the Palestinian. He must make the present; unlike the Stendhalian or Dickensian case, the present is not an imaginative luxury but a literal existential necessity. A scene barely accommodates him. If anything, then, Kanafani's use of the scene turns it from a novelistic device which anyone can recognize into a *provocation*. The paradox of contemporaneity for the Palestinian is very sharp indeed. If the present cannot be "given" simply (that is, if time will not allow him either to differentiate clearly between his past and his present or to connect them, it is because the disaster, unmentioned except as an episode hidden within episodes, prevents continuity), it is intelligible only as *achievement*. Only if the men can manage to pull themselves out of limbo into Kuwait can they *be* in any sense more than mere biological duration, in which earth and sky are an uncertain confirmation of *general* life. Because they must live—in order ultimately to die—the scene prods them into action, which in turn will provide writer and reader with the material for "fiction." This is the other side of the paradox: a scene is made for the novel, but out of material whose portrayal in the present signifies the psychological, political, and aesthetic result of the disaster. The scene *provokes* Abu Qais; when he achieves action because of it, he has made a readable document and, ironically, the inevitability of his extinction. The distances between language and reality are closed.

As I have said, the immediacy of Kanafani's subject matter tends to give his scenes their subtly provocative character. Yet between 1948 and 1967 some of the same urgency informs other work using the scenic method as I have described it. In Naguib Mahfouz' fiction, certainly the most magisterial of novelistic achievements in the Arab world, whether in the Trilogy (1956–57) or *Awlad haritna* (1959) or the collections of short stories, episodism is everywhere apparent. The scene dramatizes *periodicity*, that is, the active historical process by which Arab reality, if it is to have existential status, must form itself. That reality's intermittent nature, which in Mahfouz' postnaturalistic phase of the early sixties has been called *al-wujudiyah al-waqi 'iyah* ("realistic existentialism"),[13] developed more and more insistently into an aesthetic of minimalism and shattering effect; its complement was, I think, the quasi-Hegelian comic drama—or rather *dramatism*, since the play was in a sense the subject of the play—*Al-farafir* (1964), by Yousef Idriss. There are similarities also between these works and Hussayn Fawzi's *Sindibad misri*, subtitled *Jawlah fi rihab al-tarikh* [Travels through the expanses of history]. Hussayn himself speaks of the cinematic techniques he uses in a book whose aim, he says, could not have been achieved before 1952: to show how Egypt is a maker of civilizations. Hussein's method is episodic, so that each incident selected as an illustration of Egypt's character is a scene confirming Egypt's historical destiny as its own self-maker.

It is worth mentioning digressively that no one who has seen an Arabic "popular" film from before 1967 can have failed to notice the central, and sometimes seemingly irrelevant, presence of the cabaret or theater scene. Nor in the popular Rihani stage comedies is the carefully prepared scene of verbal attack (*radh*), rather like a human cockfight, any less *de rigueur*. Such scenes are often dismissed as catering to some vague mass cult (of voyeurism? lower-class sensationalism?), while their obvious connection with the preciously refined *maqama* tradition passes unnoticed. This tradition is the one of formal story-telling (out of which *A Thousand and One Nights* develops), among whose characteristics is the dramatization of the tale's telling. Under the influence of a highly important event that is incompletely understood and difficult to apprehend aesthetically, the story-telling tradition tends to become highly self-conscious; the event is 1948, and art turns back on itself to become meta-art. The scene is the location of the nexus between art and its objects: it knits time and character together in an exhibited articulation. Pushed to the surface thus, articulation guarantees survival, as Scheherazade's nightly recital in *The Arabian Nights* postpones her own death. The impending, or surrounding, disaster is displaced by a human duration continuously being made; the effect is not unlike the technique in Conrad's narratives, where an important event seems always to require the setting up of a narrative occurrence such as men swapping yarns, a circle of friends listening to a story-teller, and so on.

Gamal Abdel Nasser was to make the Pirandellian motif in all this very explicit. Arab history, he wrote in his *Philosophy of the Revolution,* was like a role in search of an actor to play it or, in the terms I have been using, like a scene in search of a drama. These metatheatrical images force history into two temporalities: one, that of actuality in which the disaster has taken place, a temporality of discontinuity or rupture; and, two, a temporality constituting the scene as a site for a restorative history. Thus *that* something gets articulated, constituted, and set tends to be more important than *what* is articulated: this is a common enough motif in modern literature, where the conditions of drama or narrative are in some ways more important than the subject of narration. According to Abdullah Laroui this also happens to coincide with a motif in the history of Islam, which, he speculates, is seductive because system and structure compel individualized acts into patterns. [14]

The tension between system and occurrence underlies the tension between scene and the drama of which it is a part. For Arabic prose after 1948 the political issue underlying this tension is everywhere latent. It means, for example, that there may be no whole linking these parts, no "Arab" idea, identity, history, collectivity, destiny, drama, novel giving the diachrony of scene-events any synchronic intention, aim, structure, meaning. The present may after all be *only* that, perhaps not a consequence of the past and certainly not a basis for the future. I raise this cluster of problems here in order to emphasize the investigative character of Arabic writing during the post-1948 period. For problematic doubts did not mean stupefaction. All the evidence we have points to wide-ranging intellectual and aesthetical activity. My point is that the formal characteristics which I have been describing do not merely reflect passively on the problems: they are those problems in a very privileged, engrossing way. Thus the sustained tension between the present and either the past or the future creates the scene which, in turn, is (not a reflection of) the present in a form of raised tension with the past and the future. The dialectic is constant, and enriching.

The effects of the war of 1967 predictably were to instance, published a book entitled *Ma'na al-nakba mujada-*instance, published a book entitled *Ma'na al-nakba mujada-dan* [The meaning of the disaster renewed]. The scene was transformed from a theatrical one into an arena of fairly immediate gladiatorial struggle. The relations between spectator and action were variously defined now.

In some post-1967 works, notably those by Sadek al-Azm—and even though he was writing philosophical and/or political polemic it is hard to overlook the sheer theatricality of his performance—the author entered the arena, identified the combatants, and engaged them.[15] Such an optic took it that the war of 1967 was the first truly international war fought by the Arabs in modern times. This was a war fought as much in the media as on the battlefields; the struggle was felt to be *immediately historical* because it was fought simultaneously in the scenes created by actuality and those created by television, radio, newspapers. In this sense everything about the war was historical, just as, according to Lukács, the Napoleonic wars for the first time in European history had engaged the masses in a truly international way.[16] Hitherto wars had been distant and exclusively the affair of armies. Now everyone was involved. Everything thought or written about the war had the status of historical act; whether as a soldier, a writer, or an ordinary citizen, the Arab became part of a scene which, in the case of al-Azm, was claimed to have been largely the creation of passivity, backwardness, the mediations of custom, religion, and ossified tradition. Therefore the only progressive role to be played was that of an activist-author forcing the Arab to recognize his role in the struggle. No one could be, or really ever was, a spectator: the present was not a project *to be* undertaken; it was now. Whether he discussed the *fahlawi* personality, or the consternation caused in Egypt by the visitation of the Virgin, al-Azm saw the Arabs fighting themselves, and, whether they admitted it or not, he was going to prove it to them by fighting them.

The didactic, even pedantic, quality of al-Azm's prose should be seen as part of a burgeoning general interest in precision. The Egyptian critic Shukry Ayyad has said that beyond the first cries of anguish and denial after June 10, writers began to make it their task to render the exact detail of everyday life. They hoped thus to diagnose those causes of the defeat that could be remedied. Yet Ayyad believed that a perhaps unforeseen effect of such writing was actually to intensify the anguish (*qalaq*) of modern man in the technological age. Some writers therefore treat Arab reality as a marvelous enigma (*lughz bari'*) to be deciphered; others draw attention to the aesthetic skill with which reality was being portrayed. [17] And indeed the proliferation of "absurdist" drama and narrative testifies to Ayyad's point. In Raymond Gebara's *Taht ri'ayit zaqqur* the scene is an occasion for mockery; as in al-Azm's work, quotations from "correct" sources are employed as starting points for sarcastic dissociation. Hamlet becomes a whining Arab boy, and so on. Yet unlike al-Azm's writing as a whole, which has an active intellectual integrity, Gebara's aesthetic of self-deprecating quotation conceals quietism of the most extreme sort. And it is this quietism that finally makes for the differences between intellectual activism and absurdist pastiche; the former is self-criticism based on revolutionary presupposition; the latter is not. Al-Azm's books are linked directly to the political importance of radical analysis and of radical movements, the Palestinian groups in particular. In their verbal form, as well as in their fate, intellectual activism and absurdist pastiche are rejections of the present: for both, the scene is most usefully understood as immediate history in spite of Arab failure. Thus a new paradox, one that turns the Arab into a world-historical individual because of his specialized talent for ineptitude, is born.

Since 1967, however, there has been no unanimity on the principal thesis which that disaster supposedly proved, the existence of a collective Arab identity. While it is true that the war involved the Arabs as a whole, the very particularism spurring the writer to capture every detail of life also led him to make precise differentiations between, say, local experience and collective experience. In a curious way, therefore, the rise in prominence of Palestinian writers after 1967 (Mahmoud Darwish, Samih el-Kassem, Kanafani, Fadwa Touqan, and others), a tendency which accompanied the enormous dissemination of political interest in specifically Palestinian activity, was only one aspect of the change that also produced a more intense focus upon the distinctions between the varieties of Arab experience. This, I think, is notably true in Egypt. Certainly the most brilliant writing produced during the past generation, Mahfouz' collection of short stories and playlets *Taht al-mizalla* (1969), was written in the months immediately following the 1967 June War. As with most of Mahfouz' other work, the collection is composed of short scenes, although now the scene has a special new character: instead of being part of a prospective continuity in the making, each individual scene is shot through with the desolation of extreme, and hence Egyptian, loneliness. The scene therefore is a sort of national clinical process. Things take place with the utmost medical clarity, yet their general opacity, their terrifying impingement on every ordinary citizen, their defiance of ordinary, lay understanding, the swift succession of inexplicably triggered events, all these cut off the action (always minutely Egyptian) from understanding or, more interestingly, from the possibility of a universal Arab explanation. Mahfouz' world turns Egypt into a vast hospital whose boundaries are the various military fronts, and whose patients are, equally, soldiers and citizens. The author presents his cases silently; no explanations or apologies are given. A curious, perhaps obsessive, theme in this collection as well as in Mahfouz' 1973 novel of no-war no-peace Egypt, *Hubb taht al-matar*, is the cinema. The scenes in which films are being made, where directors are being sought for their help in solving some specially difficult problem of interpretation, in which citizens are seen changing into actors, are common. When Egyptian involvement in Palestine or Yemen is mentioned, it is always by way of journalism or the cinema. Arab problems must be mediated by the layers of Egyptian reality that surround everyday life like the walls of a clinic, or the protection of a cinema studio.

Hanging over all the writing produced after 1967 is, nevertheless, the sense of profound disappointment. This is true of Mahfouz' work, of Halim Barakat's fiction, of al-Azm's polemics, and, indeed, of all those works either portraying or explaining the sudden speed of the disaster, its astonishing surprise, and the catastrophic lack of Arab resistance. No Arab can have been immune from the feeling that his modern history, so laboriously created—scene by scene—would prove so easy to brush aside in the test. The almost incredible outpouring of print after 1967 suggests a vast effort at reconstructing that history and that reality. Of necessity the first stage is the one represented in Barakat's fiction, the one that corresponds to the stage of disillusion whose classic will always be Flaubert's *L'Education sentimentale,* the great Parisian example of post-1848 European disappointment. Like Flaubert, Barakat, in *Days of Dust,* examines responses in Beirut to an Arab political calamity which ought to be understood in terms of failure, not in those of an enemy's victory. Unlike Flaubert, Barakat shows a genuine kindness to his cast of actors; he has none of Flaubert's bitter indictment of an entire generation. Whereas in *L'Education sentimentale* sentiment and fantasy are associated with the impotent failure at which Frederic Moreau and Deslauriers finally arrive, in Barakat's novel sentiment is employed to heighten the human poignancy of the disaster. For Barakat disappointment and dislocation can always be made intelligible if they are commented on with reference to justificatory passion. The images of sea and fire, as well as the sequences using the *Flying Dutchman* figure, are instruments of clarification employed to increase the disaster's universality, and its tragic shades.

Barakat's use of the scene shares with Mahfouz' technique the interest in intense particularity; indeed, it shares with Barakat's classic study (done jointly with Peter Dodd) of the 1967 Palestinian refugee exodus, the practiced sociologist's focus on those minutiae of everyday life that compose man's large-scale activity.[18] Yet Barakat's scene is dominated by the almost hateful sequence of six days. This short succession of moments dominates the action off-stage, but in the novel Barakat amplifies these days into a wide-ranging geographical and emotional voyage. His blurring of space-time distinctions, the montage effect of rapid scene-change, the carefully chosen cross-section of characters from Beirut to Amman to the West Bank, all these argue a sometimes uncertain balance between the social scientist's deliberateness and the novelist's inventiveness. Unlike both Flaubert and Mahfouz, Barakat takes, I think, a decidedly softer position on Arab contemporaneity in the throes of a major disaster. For him, the scene is an arena for continual struggle. Even though Arab history is a repetition of Biblical history, Barakat's principal character, Ramzy, judges it also as a field for potential victory. There is none of that bitter attitude toward repetition that animates Flaubert's work or Marx's *18th Brumaire of Louis Napoleon* or, for that matter, Mahfouz' post-1967 work. For in the end Barakat is a novelist of good will; and this is his interest.

If I say good will and not vision, I mean this as no negative judgment of Barakat. As his latest sociological work shows, he is increasingly concerned with what seems to be an inherent resistance in particular Arab societies to coherent unity.[19] Good will is genuine patriotic involvement truly baffled by the complexity of forces flowing through, but not wholly composing, everyday Arab reality. Perhaps no novelist today can undertake a synoptic view— or at least not with the instruments hitherto developed from the novel. In Europe and America it is true that the novel played a crucial (and even conservative) role in the coalescing of society around itself. Yet that role was confined primarily to the nineteenth century; the authoritative vision of realistic fiction was superseded in a way by the new knowledge available in psychology, sociology, ethnology, and linguistics. The Arab writer confronts the very complex interweaving of society and contemporary knowledge with an even more complex mixture of styles, backgrounds, and predilections. The novelist will doubtless register his own crisis as a novelist facing the subject matter and its challenges. But in this task he starts from the same point as every other Arab intellectual; that point is nothing other than the forward position leading forward, the region's collective reality. Ultimately, then, the crises of Arab writers are precisely, and more so than elsewhere, those of the society at large. As this recognition is increasingly diffused, the unsung heroic role played by the Arab writer since 1948 will surely receive its due acknowledgment. In the meantime one can do no less than read with the care and urgency of an involved writer.

NOTES

1. For the broadest and most literate examination of the connection between the novel as an institution and society see Harry Levin, *The Gates of Horn* (New York, 1963); on the general problem of literary form and social reality see Lucien Goldmann, *Le Dieu caché* (Paris, 1955), and his *Recherches dialectiques* (Paris, 1959).

2. Georg Lukács, *The Theory of the Novel*, tr. Anna Bostock (Cambridge, Mass., 1971), p.88.

3. "Molestation and Authority in Narrative Fiction" in *Aspects of Narrative*, ed. J. Hillis Miller (New York, 1971).

4. See also Le Gassick's articles: "A Malaise in Cairo: Three Contemporary Egyptian Authors," *The Middle East Journal*, Vol. 21, No. 2 (Spring, 1967); "Some Recent War-related Arabic Fiction," *The Middle East Journal*, (Autumn, 1971); "The Literature of Modern Egypt," *Books Abroad* (Spring, 1972).

5. *The Meaning of the Disaster,* tr. R. Bayly Winder (Beirut, 1956).

6. See his introduction to the collection of essays in *Sociologie de l'impérialisme* (Paris, 1971), pp. 15–63, and his interview with the Beirut quarterly *Al-Thaqafa al Arabiyah* (Spring, 1973).

7. *Thawrat al-fikr fi adabina al-hadith* (Cairo, 1965), pp. 107 ff.

8. *Adab al muqawamah* (Cairo, 1970), p. 128.

9. *Adab wa urubah wa hurriya* (Cairo, 196?), p. 100.

10. *Yawmiyyat na'ib fil aryaf* (repr: Cairo, 1965), p. 96.

11. There is an even worse sort of analysis—the kind that purports to deliver the "content" of literature as evidence of political attitudes and (this is its real intent) of the so-called Arab "mind" or "character." There is a time-honored tradition of such analyses in the West, most of them deriving from the profession of "Orientalism." More recently, in Israel and the United States, cultivated racialism of this sort is to be found in many places, mostly academic and governmental. A typical and influential example is Gen. Yehoshafat Harkabi's *Arab Attitudes toward Israel,* tr. Misha Louvish (New York, 1972).

12. *Rijal fil shams* (Beirut, 1963), pp. 7–8 (my translation).

13. Ragai al-Naqqash, *Udaba' mu'asirun* (Cairo, 1967), pp. 153 ff.

14. "Pour une méthodologie des études islamiques: L'Islam au miroir, de G. von Grunehaum," *Diogène,* No. 83 (July-September, 1973), p. 41.

15. This is especially true of two works produced shortly after the 1967 war: *Al naqd al thati ba'ad al hazima* (Beirut, 1969) and *Naqd al fikr al dini* (Beirut, 1969).

16. *The Historical Novel,* tr. Hannah and Stanley Mitchell (London, 1962), pp. 24 ff.

17. *Al adab fi alam mutaghayyir* (Cairo, 1971), pp. 147–48.

18. *River without Bridges: A Study of the Exodus of the 1967 Arab Refugees* (Beirut, 1969).

19. See his recent study "Social and Political Integration in Lebanon: A Case of Social Mosaic," *The Middle East Journal,* Vol. 27, No. 3 (Summer, 1973).

TRANSLATOR'S FOREWORD

THE ENGLISH-SPEAKING WORLD so abounds in talented fiction-writers that it seems necessary to justify the translation of novels from other languages into English. In this case such justification is easily made. The present novel treats an international and intercommunal crisis and exposes emotions and motivations that, by their very nature, demand expression by an insider, someone personally involved. In the West we can learn much intellectually from our news media about the historical background, current events, and personalities that affect the Arab-Israeli situation, but we have little opportunity to gain a true appreciation of the personal feelings of the antagonists. If anything, we have from our news media, and from Jews and Zionists within our society, greater opportunity to understand the Israeli point of view; this novel provides us with rare and valuable insights into the nature, strength, and direction of Arab feelings. Though reflecting constantly the author's sensitivity to the personal tragedies of war, it emphasizes the determination and dedication on the part of the Arabs that led so inevitably to the renewed warfare of October, 1973.

Halim Barakat does not, of course, pretend to speak for all Arabs. But the range of characters he introduces and their diverse reactions to current events certainly ring true. Ramzy himself, the central figure, with all his conflicting emotions, doubts, and determination, seems to express feelings shared wherever Arabic is spoken.

The novel is both factual and autobiographical in several areas, and a few details of the life and background of the author will assist in its appreciation. Halim Barakat was born to Greek-Orthodox Arab parents in 1933 in Kafroun, a Syrian village close to the Mediterranean and near the Lebanese border. He attended schools in Lebanon, where his parents established residence when he was a child, and worked his way through the American University of Beirut. Holding degrees in sociology, he went to the United States and in 1966 obtained a doctorate in social psychology at the University of Michigan. Since that time he has been teaching at the American University and the Lebanese University. In 1972–73 he served as a research fellow at Harvard University.

Barakat began writing fiction in the fifties and has concerned himself particularly with the lot of the Palestinian refugee. Several early stories deal with the psychological strains of living in the Arab refugee camps. In 1961 he published a short novel, *Sittat Ayyām* [Six days], which may well have been the most impressive piece of Arabic fiction to that date dealing with the Palestine problem. Relating the futility of Arab efforts over a six-day crisis period to defend a seaside village against imminent Israeli invasion, the novel was harshly critical of the tradition-bound faults and absurdities in modern Arab society, still so divided by barriers of class and religion.

The present novel, too, first published in Beirut in 1969,

is critical of Arab society and reflects the mood of despair and frustration that overswept the Arab world following the 1967 defeat. Self-deception and lack of organization of the Arab governments and armies and the ineffectiveness of Arab intellectuals are shown to have been the true causes of the disaster. Israeli military skills, the use of surprise, and superior weaponry, especially air power and napalm, are depicted as easily exploiting Arab overconfidence and unpreparedness.

Following the war, the author, like the novel's central figure, traveled to Amman, where he interviewed refugees and victims of the fighting and asked them about their recent experiences. It is from these interviews, on which he has also based sociological studies, that Barakat learned of some of the events and incidents described in this novel. In some cases he has changed names and places; but most of the figures apparently represent the author's impressions of real people and actual incidents reported directly to him or in the Arabic press.

The original from which this translation was rendered appeared in Arabic under the title 'Awdat al-Ṭā'ir ilā al-Bahr [Return of the Flying Dutchman to the sea] in Beirut in 1969. This version attempts to represent closely in an acceptable English form the characters, situations, and mood of the original. Some editing of imagery has occurred, and some literary allusions and quotations from English and American literature have been omitted. Some phrases and short passages that tended to be repetitious have been dropped or condensed, and the names of characters and places simplified, while left in recognizable form.

The author and the translator wish to express their appreciation to Professor Edward Said for writing the introduction, to Linda Norris for her editorial assistance, and to Faber & Faber and Harcourt Brace Jovano-vich Inc. for permission to quote from T. S. Eliot's "The Love Song of J. Alfred Prufrock" and "The Hollow Men."

TREVOR LE GASSICK
Department of Near Eastern Studies
University of Michigan

April, 1974

PART ONE

The Threshold

JUNE 11–JUNE 20, 1967

THE WORLD CHANGED INTO WATER, and darkness covered all. The sun was extinguished, and the moon did not yet exist. To Ramzy Safady it seemed that all was taking form anew; the biblical legend was repeating itself. Earth was a desolate wasteland and there was darkness over the face of the deep; but the spirit of God did not move upon the waters.

Ramzy made his way up to the heights overlooking the basin and valley of the River Jordan. Crossing the river was forbidden. Lamentation filled the distances between him and his brothers.

There was no light, no firmament. The waters did not gather, and the earth crumbled in thirst. The land grew neither grass nor trees. The Arabs stubbornly farmed stones.

No birds flew above the children in the refugee camps.

The Arab was not made in the likeness of God, so the fish of the sea, the birds of the air, and the creatures of the land had dominion over him.

And the Arab saw all he had done and, behold, it was very bad.

Ramzy returned to Amman. He passed down al-Salt Street on his way to the heart of the city. The men's faces were bewildered and sad. He had difficulty walking on the pavement and crossing the street because of the crowds. Yet a quietness enveloped the city. This was not the Amman he had known. All the clamor of life there had died.

He gazed up at Ashrafiya, the mountain ridge above. The minaret of the great mosque rose against a blue sky adorned with small, white clouds. He longed to see his friend Pamela. Perhaps she was at the hospital or at one of the schools filled with refugees.

He ought not to have separated from the delegation.

Why was he trying to get away from it all? Not that he could, in any case. The screams followed him wherever he went: "Leave me to die!" "Leave me alone!"

Taha Kanaan's screams had pursued Ramzy ever since he had arrived in Amman, on the day after the war had ended. Ramzy had walked through the streets of the city and had gone from one hospital to another. Taha Kanaan's napalm-burned face stuck to him. Ramzy wished the sea would surge up to this land and take with it everything in its path. He wished the sea could wash the dust from his face.

It did not matter that it was growing dark. He would climb to the highest peak of Ashrafiya and watch the stars. The weeping of the refugee children would rise up to him, and he would listen to it. He would not fear that their songs, like the songs of the Sirens, might bewitch him. He would not fear that his country's grief might infect him.

He had arrived in Amman as part of a delegation of doctors, professors, and students. Pamela and his friend Bashir were treating those who had been burned by napalm. Ramzy was observing, listening, questioning, and taking pictures. He was absorbed in this frightened, defeated world about him.

He watched the blank faces of the refugees. The people had been severed from their faces, which were pallid and abandoned. Their eyes were dazed, their lips clamped. They were still experiencing the first terror that followed the shock.

The humor had disappeared from the face of Umm Rizk. She no longer wanted her husband to tell stories. Khalid Abdel Halim had brought his flute with him from the village of Sabastia, but it would be a long time before he would again breathe into it some of his spirit. Taha Kanaan sat in bed in the hospital, unconscious of his burns. He was thinking how his daughter Labiba had died of napalm burns before she was four years old. His elder daughter, Adla, was dead too. Their burns had been too deep, down to the bone. He was worried about his son, Darwish. Taha's shoulders were sagging beneath the burden of the world. And a few days before he had not heard of napalm! Now there was nothing on earth closer to him than its fire, clinging to his bones.

People looked like mummies as they crossed the streets. No one seemed to want to sleep, eat, drink, talk, or smile. No one wanted to sell or buy.

Ramzy had said to Pamela, "The Arabs are passing through purgatory."

"And what are their sins?"

"Many. But ignorance is the most important."

"Maybe the war will prove a purgatory for the Arabs."

"You think they will reach paradise on earth?"

"The legend says whoever enters purgatory must surely reach the earthly paradise. Purgatory is a journey of hope."

The breeze had played with her long blond hair, like ripe wheat awaiting harvest beneath a burning sun.

She had said, trying to lift his spirits, "It's a necessary stage. They'll pass through it."

Her efforts to alleviate his deep depression had failed. He still felt, like everything around him, somehow fragmented and confused. He was overwhelmed by the bitter reality.

Taha's cries pursued him: "Let me die! Leave me alone!"

Ramzy had stood before Taha's burned face, two eyes

screaming with pain. He had tried to steel himself and to accept that pain was the way to life, that Taha was searching for life in the hell-fires of death. It struck him that Taha was in fact searching for either death or life, but was finding neither.

A reporter had come up to Bashir and, pointing to Taha, had asked: "Burned with a napalm bomb?"

"Can't you see for yourself?"

"I want to make sure. I never saw anything like this before. Is he a soldier or a civilian?"

"Civilian."

"I heard that a number of his family were hit."

"Besides himself—his son and his two daughters."

"How are they?"

"His daughters are dead. He and his son survived."

Now Ramzy slowly made his way up the mountainside, stumbling beneath the weight of the past. He acknowledged his sins and wanted to bear these terrible punishments. He was announcing his repentance and accepting his torments. He would free himself from his sins and his weaknesses. He would leave behind him those oceans of despair and seek light from the stars. With the dew, he would wash the tear stains from his face; and he would carry a burning stick of incense to protect himself from evil.

He was a traveler uncertain of his way. He was frightened and alone, and he cast no shadow on the world. He wished he had the ability to look at himself, to see the truth with clarity. He wished he could peer into all those towns piled about him, bandage their wounds, make friends with all their people, and rise in revolt with them against their oppressors. He did not want to hear moans, but shouts. He did not want to see surrender, but defiance. His feet felt lighter as he advanced, the stone weights rolling off.

The closer he climbed to the top of the mountain ridge, the freer he became.

He looked out toward the sun and turned to the left. His anger turned to love, his love to anger. The two mixed. He opened his eyes wide, then shut them tight.

He came across two heads carved in a stone wall, supporting one another.

One of them asked him, "Where are you from?"

"I have dragged my body from an Arab coast. It would be pointless to tell you who I am. My name is not well known. I almost forget it myself and doubt if I exist. I was exiled when still young."

"And what happened to the great rivers?"

"They dried up."

"In Rome we used to eat their fruits."

"The fruits are dead, and Rome is dead."

The second head asked in surprise, "What, Rome is dead?"

"Ever since the Christians occupied her."

"You're a Muslim!"

"No, I reject and am rejected. I'm not a believer, but not an atheist either."

"You're a communist?"

"No, but not a capitalist."

"You're a rightist?"

"No."

"You're a leftist?"

"No."

"Well, what are you then?"

"I am not a part of anything. All I know of myself is that I reject and am rejected."

The second head said, "You'll spend a long time in purgatory, then."

"I prefer that to heaven or hell."

"To heaven?"

"Yes. A place without sin would be sickening—a place without conflict or crisis."

"You enjoy conflict and crisis?"

"Absolutely."

"So why don't you stop moving up to the summit?"

"I dislike standing still and enjoy movement."

"You'll only harvest straw."

"Probably."

Ramzy left the two heads and continued on his way. He walked on round the mountain, climbing up to its top. He spoke aloud, to prove that he was not dreaming. But he could not be certain that the voice he heard was his own. His love for high places possessed him, and he was no longer afraid. But confusion was building inside his head. There were spirits all around, and each was a mirror reflecting the others. Some of the masks were coming off the faces.

One spirit asked him, "Tell us about the world."

"The world is barren, even to the core."

Groans were emitted: "The world is blind!"

"True. That description is to a great extent accurate."

"You seem to take pride in that. You are gloating at the world."

"I'm neither proud nor gloating; but I can't ignore the facts. And it's my countless questions that distress me."

"It seems you lack the inner strength to control your passions and the world around you."

"Quite likely!"

Ramzy could feel the warm rays of the sun giving him life once again.

The summit was visible on the horizon, but he would need to travel long and far before arriving there. What mattered was that he was on the way, and that he could see it. Now he cast a shadow. He wanted it to grow and spread and give shade to the world. He enjoyed discussion with those spirits traveling toward that summit where the earthly paradise was to be found.

Ramzy visited the schools and hospitals where the refugees from the West Bank were piled. They had arrived in a daze, unable to comprehend what had happened to them. Taha thought he was in some frightful dream and kept expecting to wake up and discover that all the time he had been in his own bed, that there had been no war, that his family had not been burned in napalm. Time was passing slowly, but his hope that he was dreaming was fading rapidly.

Bashir attended to another victim from Jerusalem. The man seemed only semiconscious and kept repeating words that no one could understand: "No! No! Amina! Oh! Oh! The river! The river!"

The doctor examined him and saw that it was hopeless. The napalm had burned through all the layers of his skin, leaving the bones visible in a number of places. Bashir stared at the bones of the man's face and hands. He had never seen anything so frightful in all his life. The man's blackened face could be that of any human being; all its distinctive features had been obliterated.

A bitter silence overwhelmed all. The world was water, and darkness covered everything.

A dove descended from the skies in the form of a napalm bomb on a magus searching for peace on earth.

PART TWO

Voices Surge and The South Wind Rages

JUNE 5–JUNE 10, 1967

THE FIRST DAY

Thunder in the Voices of Children

RAMZY SAFADY had been expecting something to happen at any time. His feelings on the morning of Monday, June 5, 1967, were no different from those of the previous two days. Something had to happen. The crisis had reached the point of no return. He was aware, of course, that some backing down might occur, bringing a temporary lull. His feelings today remained mixed and confused. The Arabs seemed on the verge of some great adventure, and they clearly had little freedom of choice between facing or fleeing from it.

He felt somehow like the skipper of a small ship about

to embark on an ocean that has never been crossed. But the thought of being the captain of a ship deeply troubled Ramzy, for he had no authority and no idea where the rudder was nor who had charge of it. In any event, he had supported, and still did, the move of blocking the Straits of Tiran, off Sharm al-Sheikh. Arab public opinion was in support of that action.

That simple word, *support,* gives no idea of the enormous emotional force that had overwhelmed the Arab world. The newspapers, magazines, radio broadcasts, and television had exulted in that action. The Arabs felt a sense of triumph. They were establishing once again that they did have some will and courage to demand their rights, to refuse submission to the will of others who ignored their rights and feelings. They rejected, and therefore they existed.

These thoughts pleased Ramzy, but, at the same time, they annoyed him. All this meant he had to abandon those petty pleasures that had come to dominate his life. Now was the time to cut his ties with Fatina and her crowd. Ever since he had come to know her, he had spent most of his evenings with them—discussing sex, and drinking and eating. He had been surprised, and so had the others, that he enjoyed talking candidly about sex, and also that he sometimes drank too much. Ever since he had stopped seeing Najla, cut loose from his family, begun living alone in an apartment, and bought a new car, he had discovered a pleasure in flirting with married women. He had been amazed how many responded quickly to him; their lives were unbelievably empty. He had been particularly surprised at Fatina.

But Ramzy had tired of these discussions and parties and had been looking for some opportunity to get back to talking politics and philosophy with his old friends. Now was his chance.

He was busily contemplating this as he made his way to his office at the university. It made him happy to notice the change in the facial expressions of his colleagues and students, who were, perhaps for the first time, taking a real interest in what was happening to the Arab world. Their behavior showed how much they wanted to transcend the peripheral, uninvolved nature of their lives.

Picking up his books and notes, Ramzy went off to his class. He had enjoyed the last discussion with his students on the relationships between man's position within the social and class structure and his political behavior. Today the discussion moved off to political symbolism. The last thing Ramzy said was, "In the beginning was the word. It is man who creates symbols, but they come to dominate him. Man gives things their significance, but they attain a power of their own and become, to a large extent, independent of him, gaining as much influence over him as he has over them. Man may, for example, refuse to treat his rights too lightly. And with time this refusal may become a symbol and the symbol become a *cause célèbre* and focal point for all his capacities. And for this symbol he will even go to war, if necessary."

A student came rushing in, shouting, "The war's broken out! Israel has attacked Egypt!"

A student from Damascus shouted, "Allahu Akbar, God is great," as he ran outside.

A Sudanese student said loudly, "In the beginning was the war."

Ramzy realized how futile their discussion was in relation to world events, and he wished he could now add, "Man creates war, but it becomes independent of his will and

15

re-creates him in a form that it wishes, a form that has absolute control over his old self."

The classroom emptied and the tumult outside increased. He could feel it surging in waves, stinging against his face, as he walked to his office in the company of several of his students. A foreign student asked his opinion of the war—what the outcome would be and how long it would last. He replied rather curtly; he did not feel capable of discussing anything. An Arab student asked him what would happen about the final exams, whether the teachers would take the present circumstances into consideration. Ramzy made no reply, although he felt like saying, "You miserable crow, you."

He entered his office and sat in an armchair. He got up again and looked out the window. The students were drifting to and fro, like swelling waves, and foam was rising everywhere. He sat down and stood up once more, letting his gaze wander over the booklined walls but without seeing them. What was the use of books, anyway? Tamerlane had burned the libraries of Baghdad. He took a few restless steps, then returned and sat quietly.

He stared at a map of Palestine. For twenty years he had been in exile. His roots were exposed to the air, being beaten by the heat of the sun. He simply had to go back. Yet would his exile ever end? If it was not to end now, it had to end in the future. He raised his hand to his forehead, as though searching for something he could not quite remember.

A deep depression gripped him. He knew that he ought to be thinking of ways in which he might help repel the fierce danger that was threatening the Arab world. He thought deeply. But no satisfactory answer came. He was powerless. When it came to the life or death of his country, he found himself helpless.

His friend Nadir Hamdany charged into Ramzy's office like a foaming wave, yelling happily, "War's broken out! It's war!"

Ramzy remarked coldly, "Yes, I've heard the news."

"Well, what's wrong with you? You seem depressed."

"And what's surprising in that."

"I don't understand! Not one bit. I thought you'd be burning with excitement."

Ramzy tried to explain: "I'm sorry. It's strange. I don't know how I feel. I wasn't expecting to feel this way, confused. I feel as if the world is swelling before me, while I am getting smaller."

"You're disappointing me. I would never have expected that from you."

Ramzy maintained his calm: "Deep inside me I have a great sense of hope mixed with a profound fear. The two emotions are in conflict. It's just that it's a very dangerous situation indeed, and I feel absolutely helpless."

Nadir, trying to pull Ramzy out of the mood that gripped him, insisted: "The situation is not as scary as you think. The war is in our interest. We should welcome Israel's aggression. It's chosen its own destruction."

"I don't like war."

"You make me laugh. Do you think I like war? But it's become our only hope to win back our rights. There's no doubt about that."

Ramzy respected what his friend was saying, even though he thought him overly optimistic. Nadir certainly was an expert on the whole Palestine problem, one of the few who seriously studied conditions within the Arab countries and Israel and who made comparisons between them. He had published a book on this subject and was a member of one of the Palestinian organizations. He had also followed the development of the situation in the United

Nations and in international politics. But Ramzy could not forget that the Arab world was underdeveloped and uncoordinated, living in the twentieth century only in outward appearance. The worst of it was that it possessed no will power. It could not make up its mind on anything. It did not plan. It gloried in the past and did not dream of the future. It boasted that its people were a hundred million strong.

He expressed his feelings to Nadir: "The important thing is not numbers, but quality."

"We do have quality."

"You are deceiving yourself and your nation."

"Do you deny that we have first-class experts in a number of fields?"

"No."

"Well then?"

"You are an expert in your field. Most of our friends are experts in one field or another. Yet can you tell me what they do? Where are the institutions that know how to benefit from their expertise? Who cares about them? Who wants them to have opinions? And the experts, how in fact do they work? Do they cooperate? No one cooperates with anyone else. Each one lives in his own little world. Tell me about our institutions. Tell me about the organizations and the parties. There's really nothing, nothing at all. We lack organization and teamwork. Where's our communication and intercommunication? There are no bridges between the Arab countries. There are no bridges between individuals and groups. That's the sort of people we are. We are living in the past. We sail through swamps. We eat mud. We seek sanctity from stones and graves. We bow down in prayer before the wind."

Nadir began: "Well, I agree, but—"

Ramzy cut him off: "You've got to agree, simply, without

any *buts*. You've got to remember that less than one in a thousand can do any more than look on and clap or curse, listen to broadcasts and demonstrate, while half the Israeli population wear military uniforms. True or not?"

"True," answered Nadir. He added, in mock anger: "You are underestimating the revolutionary movements—"

Ramzy cut him off again: "I am not underestimating the revolutionary movements. I do not recognize them. All we have are revolts, not social revolutions. I hope you won't mind my being frank. You are a revolutionary in politics, but a social reactionary. There's not one of us in revolt against our customs—"

This time Nadir angrily interrupted Ramzy: "I don't think this is the time to argue out these things. We should think what action we must take."

"I apologize. You are right."

They went out into the campus, where there was much confusion. The students were shouting and singing patriotic songs.

Ramzy was surprised by Pamela Anderson, who came up to him and said, "Hello, Ramzy."

"I didn't expect to see you here."

"All the shouting attracted me. What are they saying?"

"Are you alone?"

"Yes, alone."

"Where is he?"

"I don't know. I think he left."

"Left?"

This news pleased Ramzy. He had been expecting it ever since his friend Dr. Bashir Mansoor had introduced him to Pamela and her husband, Walter. Bashir had told him they were artists traveling around the world, but with

19

very little money. Walter had complained to a doctor of
a disorder that the doctor believed to be psychosomatic.
Pamela's friend Kathy had told Ramzy that Pamela and
Walter were not getting along and that they were always
arguing. Once Ramzy had invited her to a fish dinner
in a seaside restaurant. They had played tennis together
and had gone swimming together at a quiet beach.

Pamela again asked what the students were shouting,
and he hesitated before replying. She smiled awkwardly.
He realized she might think he did not trust her, and
so he did translate some of the shouts.

GREAT CROWDS of Jericho people swarmed around Taha
Kanaan. For the past two days, he had been trying to
organize the popular resistance and civil defense groups.
He had managed to prepare a list with the names of
more than 650 volunteers. Young men were streaming
into the town hall to register. Everyone seemed to want
to donate blood, and a number of families had offered
their refrigerators to store the blood. Also, Taha Kanaan
had managed to acquire 100 rifles. He had tried to get
more—he had wanted at least 650—but without success.
He had failed and had been very angry. He distributed
the hundred rifles equally among four quarters of Jericho.

Deep silence descended when news spread of the attacks
against Egypt. Something had to be done. The silence
was dispelled as soon as it was learned that King Hussein
had declared war. The crowds seemed transformed into
masses of blazing fire.

Taha Kanaan addressed them: "Each one of us has
been waiting for these words. It is what we wanted the
king to say, and we are delighted."

The crowds lifted Taha Kanaan and carried him through the streets of Jericho. Their shouts rose in the air. The children's voices were thunder in a clear sky. The men discharged their guns into the air, while the crowds trilled for joy.

IN JERUSALEM, Azmy Abdel Qadir had become hoarse only an hour after war had broken out. This was the battle he had been waiting for since 1948. He had participated in that war, which had stopped suddenly and for reasons unknown to him. During the intervening period he had felt frustrated at not completing what had been begun. He was filled with anger, and had no outlet for it. But now he knew that he was in fact an exile and that he must continue the work he had not finished in 1948. He expected that victory would come quickly. It suddenly appeared that return to Haifa was a possibility. He could not believe it. He just could not believe it. His four children had been born in exile. He would introduce them to his childhood haunts, the ones he was always talking about. Their longing to return to Haifa was as great as his own.

He shouted out loud. Crowds of people were surging and jostling together in the streets of Jerusalem. He had not expected war to start so quickly. He was afraid that it might turn out to be a minor battle, and that when it was over life would return to its old, monotonous routine. Then Palestine would still be remote, only a dream. He could not grasp that the real battle had begun, that Palestine was to return, that he would be able to wander in the streets of Haifa, run across its beaches and into the sea. He could not believe it. He simply could not believe it.

IN SABASTIA, Khalid Abdel Halim tossed his carpenter's tool into a corner. He, too, had not expected war to begin so suddenly. The evening before, they had held a little party in his house. He had played his flute, and its melodies had seeped down to the fibers of his being. He had forgotten his problems with his mother, Salima, his responsibility to provide for his own family, for that of his sister Khayriya, and for the two little children of his sister who had been killed. The melodies had made him forget everything. He had been raised on this music. It was old, like Palestine, older than the deeply furrowed face of his mother. His mother's face and the flute were living in the hills of Palestine long before Abraham arrived from Mesopotamia.

A number of his friends had attended the party of the previous evening. He had asked his wife, Arabiya, to sit beside him and sing as he played the flute. The sound of the flute had risen and fallen and, with it, the sound of Arabiya's voice:

> Oh, to light you a victory torch to carry through the streets of Haifa.
> I've shed tears enough to soak a kerchief;
> Our villages, Zaita, East Jaffa, Jidd, and Kakoun, are worth that much.

The flute had swelled deep and low, melancholic and mournful, filling the whole world, moaning in sadness, and moving like the River Jordan and the wind over the hills of Palestine.

> I had to say good-bye, my hometown,
> Now a stranger, drying my tears on my sleeve.
> If I stay much longer away from home,

Then, oh! so hard I'll moan,
And my eyes will weep blood.

Umm Rizk's eyes had glistened. To break the mood, she laughed heartily and said to Khayriya: "Well, don't *you* be unhappy. You have no problems. Suppose you did have a husband, but one like mine, eh?" She glared over at her husband. It seemed as if he had not understood. She then began badgering him to tell everybody his favorite story, the one about the hyena and the bride. A vapid smile crept over his face. He pretended to be reluctant, but she kept insisting. At last he began, stuttering as always.

"Well, once—once upon—once upon a time—once—once there was a wedding—a wedding—a wedding. The bride—the bride rode on a horse—a horse. She rode on her horse—a horse—a fine horse—and on the way—on the way—a hyena attacked her. A huge hyena—huge—huge—just huge. So the hyena snatched her up—it snatched up the bride—the bride. It snatched her up—snatched her—and carried her off to its cave—a cave—and it started attacking her—and it attacked her—"

There was laughter all around. Umm Rizk chortled with delight and asked her husband, "What? What?"

Khalid entered the conversation: "Well, why don't you explain to everyone, then?" Explain it to them. Tell them what happened."

So Abu Rizk continued: "Well, he attacked her—that is, he attacked her—by that I mean that he, well, attacked her. Anyway, the bridegroom heard of it—he got to hear of it—so he took his gun. Yes, he took his gun—a rifle—and he went off to the cave. And he let loose at the hyena—yes, he shot at him—but he didn't hit him. And the hyena attacked him—he went for him. He shot again—but he didn't hit him. So the bridegroom ran—he ran and ran—and he climbed—yes, he climbed—up a tree—he climbed up—and up—and up. And so there was the hyena, stuck at the tree. Stuck right there."

"What do you mean, Abu Rizk 'stuck'?" Khayriya asked. He explained: "I mean stuck. Just stuck. He stuck there. The hyena pissed on his tail. He pissed on his tail. He sprayed and sprayed and hit the bridegroom. He got him. The bridegroom was put under a spell, right under a spell. So he climbed down. He climbed down from the tree. He came right down, and he followed the hyena, closer and closer. But then the bridegroom's head hit a rock and was split right open. The blood streamed down, streamed down, down, down. Then he came to, came out of the spell, and he shot the hyena. The hyena dropped dead. The groom snatched up the bride, snatched her right up, and attacked her and made love to her. The bridegroom made love to the bride. He attacked the bride and made love to her legally. Legally. He did it legally. He did it honestly and cleanly."

IN BEIRUT, Ramzy Safady was contemplating the same old Palestinian fable, how his country was a bride abducted by Zionism. The Palestinians had fought in 1948 to retrieve their bride, had fired shots but had not struck the hyena. Then, dazed and spellbound, they had left their bride in the cave and had climbed the tree of the Arab states. Now again they attacked the hyena; they had to save their bride. She was theirs, both by law and by love. But would they again become spellbound, dazed?

Ramzy saw one of his students, Basim, coming toward him, walking jauntily, so happy that his feet scarcely seemed to touch the ground.

Ramzy asked him, "Well, what do you think?"

"Victory. It means victory, Dr. Safady."

"Let's hope so."

"It's been a long journey. My family fled from Acre when I was six. It's been a very long journey, but now Acre is on the horizon."

Ramzy did not know what made him ask, "Have you had training in the use of firearms, Basim?"

"No. I'm afraid not."

"And do you believe we will win the war?"

"Well, of course, naturally. Israel is just a cardboard box protected by the Americans and the British. But this time they won't dare to intervene. Russia is lying in wait for them. Russian destroyers shadow the Sixth Fleet units all the time. And don't forget, Dr. Safady, that we are a hundred million Arabs."

Ramzy thought it best to stop posing questions that inspired doubt rather than faith. But doubts crept into his mind whenever he talked with anyone so zealous, yet he himself became enthusiastic whenever he talked with a skeptic. Why was that? He, too, was confused. He doubted and believed, yet his feelings of doubt and conviction rarely could take hold of facts. What he felt depended on the nature of the conversation or the person he was talking to. The fact was he did not know whether to be enthusiastic or skeptical.

The clamor of voices suddenly subsided and another radio bulletin could be heard. Everyone strained toward the loudspeakers that the students had placed on the balcony of one of the buildings to carry the latest news to all those crowding the university grounds. The announcer informed them enthusiastically, "A few moments ago Cairo announced that forty-four enemy aircraft have been shot down!"

The voices swelled into a roaring tide of jubilation. Ramzy felt a quiver run through his body. He saw that the hairs on his arms were standing erect, like spears. The students' shouts were penetrating to his very depths.

The thought struck Ramzy that his country was like the *Flying Dutchman,* the shouts of the students like those of the sailors when they sighted land. He had been listening the previous day to Wagner's opera about an enchanted ship unable to reach harbor, sailing the seas till eternity. The captain had sworn that he would circle round a mountainous peak guarded by fierce gales even if he had to sail on till judgment day. The gods, or the devils, were angry when they heard his oath and condemned him to sail on in exile forever. He could break the spell only by finding a woman true to him till death. The *Flying Dutchman* was permitted to return to land once every seven years so that he might search for such a woman. But every time he visited land he would return to sea even more despairing and disillusioned, more depressed than ever by his exile and his fruitless wanderings. He had suffered nameless tortures on the lonely and desolate seas until his body had become his death shroud. Both death and life rejected him. His suffering was as deep as the seas on which he wandered. His ship bore treasures beyond compare, but his heart was drained of hope.

Ramzy thought of his country as a ship sailing aimlessly for a long period over seas of fear, alarm, and ignorance, unable to reach any shore. The waves tossed it to and fro, jolting its rotting planks. Its sailors, who knew nothing of seamanship, cried out from the deep. There was salt on their faces and in their voices. There was neither death nor arrival. Now more than ever before they were under the spell of their limitless wanderings, entranced by their lives themselves. They could see no death on the horizon.

They were angrier than ever that their lives were their death shrouds and that they had to bear nameless tortures without hope of release. Anger was all they had left. Let them revolt before the devils and the gods, whatever the consequences.

Ramzy felt that his country was denied death as well as life. His country was a ship without a rudder, and it pained him that most of his countrymen believed that it did have a rudder. He kept repeating to himself that his country was rudderless—yes, rudderless—but not without anger. In this anger lay its future and its significance. In any case its suffering would continue until it found someone to rescue it. Someone who would be faithful to that country till death? He was not searching for someone who would dictate orders to his people, remold them, deceive them, and go along with all those rotten institutions. He longed for a leader who would glow with defiance, one who would inspire the people to use their minds and their emotions in a dialogue with themselves and with their leaders—someone who would scream for freedom, straining every nerve and emotion in search of freedom.

But what the present leaders wanted was the acquiescence of the masses. And the masses were content to be dependent and to agree. Those who wanted to think and to search and to discuss for themselves were repressed and restricted. He hated to see his people submit to mere dreams, place all their hopes on a still-awaited leader who would drag them up from the depths of despair. They had to pull themselves up; to open like a flower, from within; to create their own leaders, bring them forth in a variety of fields; to rescue themselves by being true to themselves till death.

Like his country, Ramzy was exhausted from wandering lost, over the seas. He was tired of all the hopelessness and the loneliness. He wanted to merge with his country, for the two somehow to become one, so that the aspirations throbbing within his country would beat in him as well.

War had been declared. The *Flying Dutchman* could see land, cliffs towering in the distance. Hope was rising again. It seemed the ship could dock safely. The sailors' shouts filled the air. The cheers of the university students in Beirut acclaimed the return to Palestine. Voices were rising in all parts of the Arab states.

Taha fired a salvo into the air in Jericho.

Azmy charged ahead of the thousands in the streets of Jerusalem.

Khalid felt exhilarated. His stride lengthened. He seemed to have put on a new face. Now the seas could foam around him.

A surging, swirling motion mixed with and encompassed everything, including all the tumult filling the skies.

Ramzy noticed one of his students, Siham, sitting alone and looking very depressed. He went over and asked, "Something wrong?"

He immediately regretted having asked the question, for tears began welling in her eyes. He could not leave her, yet he did not know what to say. He could hear the noise from the crowds.

He repeated, "Something wrong?"

"My family is in Jerusalem," she replied. "I'm sorry. I shouldn't give way to my feelings like this."

"Not at all. Your feelings are very natural."

He remembered hearing a radio announcement asking all women who wished to participate in civil defense training to assemble in one of the university halls, and he told her this. She said she had put her name down and was just waiting.

How could he help? What could he do? Why was he

standing there? He was just like all the thousands around him, with no idea what to do. Just like millions of other young Arabs who listened to the news, smoked cigarettes, and got excited.

He bumped into his colleague Kamil Salama and commented, "Don't you think it's a crime we aren't able to do anything?"

"You know, you and Nadir and Bashir are all asking that question. But not me."

Ramzy felt a little angry: "I don't know how you can escape asking that question."

"It's very simple. As university teachers we are able to operate during peacetime. Whatever we do in wartime should be a continuation of our search for the truth. War is a passing phenomenon. My concern is with teaching and doing research. When the time doesn't seem right to do something, I just wait."

Ramzy shook his head without comment. He heard the radio announce, "Jordan and Syria have proclaimed their readiness for instant attack." A swell of shouts arose, carrying him up along with it.

Ramzy's whole body trembled when Kamil said, looking up at the balcony, "I don't know how the university can permit them to do that."

Kamil was gazing up at the loudspeakers which, at that moment, reported Cairo's announcement that all the Arab frontal commands had begun moving toward the interior of Israel, having promised one another to meet in Tel Aviv.

The voices of the Arab university students in Beirut mixed with those of the Arabs in Jerusalem and those of the *Flying Dutchman*'s sailors. Ramzy wished his voice could rise up high, like all the rest. He shivered again. His country was facing a test. He recalled a classroom discussion on the ideas of Arnold Toynbee. Challenge and response. The vitality, capacity, and potential, or, rather, the resoluteness, of a nation become apparent in its manner of response to a challenge. Palestine was not just a "problem" for the Arabs; it was a criterion of their state of advancement and their capacity to respond to challenges. They had to stand firm and confront the test. The results were important, but the attitude more so. They had to dive into the fray, to take risks and face the storm. If his country were to hesitate to face the test today, with the excuse of being weak or incapable, then it would never face it in the future.

He could scarcely contain his joy when it was announced that Jordanian forces had taken Mount Scopus, overlooking Jerusalem, and that there was hand-to-hand fighting in the city's streets. The confrontation had begun. Suddenly, he was frightened. He actually shivered. Images of the fighting were coming to his mind. He saw bullets piercing a skull behind a wooden shutter. The cannons were roaring, the machine guns rattling and spitting fire into eyes. Bayonets. The wall of a building tumbled down. Next came the roof. The family was in there, beneath the rubble. Legs were leaping over bodies strewn in the middle of an ancient lane. A Roman soldier swaggered on his horse. Achilles charged through Troy and found himself face to face with Hector. Gilgamesh aimed his arrow at the chest of the wild bull. Enkidu's body fell as though struck by a thunderbolt.

In Jerusalem, Azmy fired his weapon.

From somewhere on the border, King Hussein announced, "The decisive battle, which the Arab nation has awaited for so long, has now begun."

In Jericho, Taha screamed, "God is great!"

The border town of Qalqilya, crouched and ready to

spring like a lion, roared when it heard the call. It was always threatened, its body bearing many wounds.

Ramzy remembered that Abdel Rahman, a student of his, had told him that his house in Zaita was exactly on the border, while his uncle's house was across the border. "Our house faces theirs. I stand in front of our house and look over at my cousin. We exchange looks but don't say a word. That's no life, Dr. Safady. A number of times I felt like leaping over the barrier. I just didn't care whether the bullets got me or not. But then I always hesitated, and thought of the future."

No doubt by now he had jumped across the border. Ramzy felt anguished at the thought that the bullets might well have penetrated Abdel Rahman's body.

This war was a threshold of the future not merely for Abdel Rahman but for Ramzy and Taha and Azmy and for all those who had been uprooted in 1948. Death was better than exile.

Ramzy returned to his office. He wondered what he should do. The telephone rang, and he slowly picked up the receiver. He heard the voice of Fatina.

"Listen, Ramzy, I've got to see you."

"Well, I don't know."

"What do you mean, you don't know? I've got to see you."

"When?"

"This evening."

"You haven't heard about the curfew?"

"What curfew? Why?"

He was amazed she had not heard that war had begun, and so he told her. She stopped talking. She did not know what to say.

He asked, "Didn't Mansur tell you?"

"No. I don't believe he knows. We don't talk much these

days, anyway. Our life together has become unbearable."

"You must try. I believe that he is a good person."

"That's not enough. I do try. I do try. I swear it. But whenever I try, I just feel that I despise him."

"You must try. You never felt that you despised him before."

"Do you want to get rid of me?"

Her question took him by surprise. He tried to deny it, but without success. He was relieved when she said, "Hang on a moment. Just wait. He wants me."

"He's there with you?"

"Yes."

"What's he doing?"

"He's taking a bath. He wants me to scrub his back."

"You scrub his back for him?"

"Why certainly. His mother used to. She scrubbed his back for him till the day she died. He got married because he needed a woman to scrub his back. Listen now, when will I see you?"

"I'm really sorry. I just don't know. We are in a state of war. I'll get in touch when I have a chance."

"You've found some other woman?"

He tried to deny it. She hung up.

He remembered her legs. She never resisted when he approached her. Sometimes she seemed to resist, but he knew that it was only an attempt to quicken his interest.

The radio reported that the Palestine Liberation Organization was reminding everyone: "It's our duty to get to work, put on our weapons, and dig trenches with our fingernails, because zero hour has struck."

It occurred to Ramzy that the streets of Lebanon were filled with trenches dug by the rain, and that the nails of the young people were all manicured and painted.

The sun was about to plunge into the sea. He got in

his car and drove to his apartment. He climbed the rickety stairs and stood on the balcony, looking out at the airport. He had never realized it was that close. Everything was quiet and at a standstill.

He went inside and busied himself painting the lightbulbs blue. The war might last a long time. His mind wandered to Fatina.

He listened to the radio. Patriotic verses. Songs. "Today, today, and not tomorrow, let the bells chime our return to Palestine."

But Ramzy could hear no bells.

"Fight, fight, O heroes, for today is the day of war."

He stretched out in an armchair.

THE INHABITANTS of the village of Neby Samwil went out into the fields and caves to hide from the flying bullets and shells. They ran like hedgehogs suddenly aware of having no quills. The din of the tanks and planes penetrated their bones and settled in their joints. The cries of the children reverberated through the caves. Sabry Mahmud kept trying to quiet his baby daughter. He was not afraid. He wanted to think. Why was it he had no weapons? Why had he run away? Why was he hiding? Why was he not fighting? He despised himself, despised his country, despised his mother for bearing him. His daughter was quiet now, asleep. There was no war as far as she was concerned. She did not know what was happening to her country. If only he did not know.

UMM MAHIR, in the village of Bayt Hanina, feared for her son. Her husband was a soldier engaged in the fighting, while she remained with her seven-year-old son, Mahir.

He did not seem scared. He wanted to know what "war" was and how his father was fighting. She sent for her husband's sister, and the three of them enjoyed each other's company. The sister told Mahir stories about war. She delighted him with a story about the Zeer, the ancient folk-hero. Then she told him another story, about his father. The boy felt proud, but his mother remained sad. She was thinking of her husband, over on the border in Qalqilya.

NIMA ABDEL RAHIM sat with her father, mother, little sister Ayisha, and friend Fathiya on the balcony of their new house in Bayt Nuba. Their faces showed nothing but composure, even though they could hear the noise of bullets and guns, and could watch the gunfire beneath them shooting off toward Jerusalem. They felt that the Arabs would win the war in a short period. The father, a retired military officer, had assured them that the Arabs would be victorious quickly and that there was no danger of explosions in Bayt Nuba. Nima wished her fiancé were there with them to witness the Arab victory, instead of in Frankfurt, alone, where he would just hear about it.

THE PEOPLE OF JERICHO were astonished at the number of planes overhead, flying very low, swooping past in a constant stream. Their noise shook the walls of the houses. They could not possibly be Arab planes. They dropped explosives without any opposition. The townspeople were terror-stricken. Taha Kanaan stayed in the city hall organizing the resistance; he did not go home. He scarcely thought about his family. They probably had gone off into the fields like so many other families. He had promised his daughter Adla a party for her graduation from the secondary school. No doubt she would understand. Victory would be the finest present she had ever received.

IT WAS NOW OBVIOUS to Azmy Abdel Qadir that far more than a minor skirmish was under way. He was delighted that it was a real war. He would go back to Haifa. But he was annoyed that Israeli planes could fly over Jerusalem without meeting any strong opposition. He was filled with pride when the Arab army regained Mount Scopus. But then the glow faded from his eyes, and anger came to take its place. Shortly after the Jordanian troops took the ridge, the planes appeared and began plastering the troops mercilessly. The bombing was continuing still. Azmy burned with rage that he was not face to face with the enemy. He had a machine gun and longed to use it. Let the enemy advance! Just let them come!

THE NEIGHBORS HAD ARRIVED to spend the evening with Khalid Abdel Halim. It was a pity the lights had to be out. They all felt a little proud because Sergeant Major Abu Daham had come by to reassure them, pointing out safety precautions they all should take. Everyone was afraid of him and yet, at the same time, had confidence in him. He was severe and uncompromising, rather hard. His being there, even for a short time, made them feel secure. There was not a soul in the village who could face up to Abu Daham without flinching. His eyes were like an eagle's, his face like a rock.

But Khalid was not awed by the man, for he had learned that Abu Daham had a taste for wine and liquor. Khalid would secretly invite him in for a drink and was always amazed at what the man could consume without much effect. Once Abu Daham had invited him to his place, which was inside an ancient fortress. He took him up a winding corridor with passages leading off in other directions. Khalid was quite apprehensive. Then Abu Daham stopped at an ancient door and unlocked it with a huge key. He pushed the door open, and its squeaking echoed through the corridors. They went inside. Khalid kept peering at the room's single window and its iron bars. Abu Daham returned to the door and made sure it was shut. Then he hurried over to an old table near the wall, opened a drawer, and took out a bottle of liquor. They both had a drink. Abu Daham drank very rapidly. He polished off the first glass in a flash, then poured another and drank it. He began chatting about his family and mentioned that he had not seen them for six months. Then he showed Khalid some photos of them. His face spread into smiles. He introduced him to his wife, his son Muflih, his daughter Bayan, and little son Mansur. Khalid asked if he had a photo of his eldest son, Daham, and the man replied that he did, but made no offer to show it to him. He gathered the photos and replaced them in the drawer. The severe, humorless look was back on his face. Nevertheless, and perhaps for the first time, Khalid felt a measure of liking for him. It did not seem that his life was as devoid of feeling as Khalid had imagined. He had discovered him to be less of a tyrant, less cruel or severe, than he appeared to be. He sensed the man was a "loner" with some dark secret in his life.

Khalid asked his sister Khayriya what was wrong, even though he knew the answer. She was sad and anxious, obviously worried. She was afraid that the war might last a long time, that something might happen to her or to her son, Tariq, before her husband's return, which she had been expecting at any time. The war was crushing her hopes. He had left her only a month after their marriage and had gone to Germany. He had been reluctant to marry her, being both her cousin and the brother of Arabiya, her brother Khalid's wife. Her mother and his had arranged it all. He had written often during the first year, but his letters became less and less frequent and now she rarely heard from him. She had written him threatening divorce and at the same time reminding him that his son, Tariq, born in his absence, was now a fine two-year-old and that she was amazed that he did not long to see him. Khalid had written, too, warning that he would divorce the man's sister, Arabiya, if he did not return to the family. He had replied that he would come back, and so Khayriya had been impatiently and eagerly awaiting him. But now the war had changed everything. She felt depressed. She held Tariq close.

Of course she did not want Khalid to divorce his wife. He loved her and she him. Khayriya had even thought of suicide. She was angriest at her mother, the cause of everything. Her mother possessed their lives as much as she did her own clothes, treating them precisely as she wished. She had arranged the loveless marriage of another daughter to an old man, with the result that the daughter had run off with a young man she did love, even after bearing her husband two sons. The mother had been furious and had incited her younger son to murder her. So it was that Khalid, the dead woman's elder brother, had become responsible for his sister's two sons as well.

Khayriya tried to forget by listening to Umm Rizk imitate her husband. She had tried to persuade him to repeat some of his stories but he had resisted. So Umm Rizk began imitating him as he talked to her.

Laughter rose. Khayriya stared at the woman and

wondered how she could so make fun of her husband and yet stay with him. She had often asked her why she did not divorce him; Umm Rizk had always replied that she was happy with him. And she certainly was happier than Khayriya, in any case.

Khalid was struck by how heartily they were laughing, even though their country was at war. But they were going to win, so why not laugh? Nevertheless he sensed a bitter silence beginning to move over the world around them.

RAMZY TRIED TO SLEEP but could not. He imagined the planes bombing Jerusalem, then climbing only to dive down at incredible speed toward Bethlehem. The thought struck him that hand-to-hand fighting would still be under way in Jerusalem, and he shuddered violently.

He went out to the balcony and looked at the airport. Some light was still escaping from the buildings there. Some of the houses had lights on, too, despite the constant warnings. People just did not take them seriously. He did not like that. And he was particularly disturbed that light from the airport was still visible. The enemy would have little trouble locating it.

Ramzy gazed up at the sky. There was nothing in the circling dome—just a deep, menacing quiet. The stars seemed quite different now. He remembered how he had loved the stars as a boy. What had become of his boyhood? There was no security in his world. He felt a little afraid. If the airport were hit, the plate glass windows of his flat would shatter. He shivered at the thought of glass breaking above his bed, splinters piercing his body, and his blood draining out till he died.

He tried to think of other things. Was it possible that in a few days he would be able to visit Palestine, the towns of Haifa, Acre, Jaffa, Nazareth, Safed, Ramla, Lydda, and Beersheba? He rested his head against the glass as he looked out at Beirut and the airport. Darkness enveloped everything. Fear had settled, too. Hope and despair were engaged in relentless battle for control of his innermost feelings. His head remained resting against the window glass. He stayed there a long time, staring out into the darkness.

THE SECOND DAY

The Sailor Returns to the Sea

Ramzy Safady awoke early on Tuesday, June 6. He turned toward the window above his head and found it intact. The airport had not been hit; the glass had not pierced his head. He tried to convince himself that he was still alive. He got up and looked into the mirror; nothing in him seemed to have changed. Head, chest, arms, legs, everything was still there. He could not see inside, of course, but his heart seemed to be beating normally.

He resumed his examination. His face was calm. He had slept well, as always. It seemed strange not to be more upset. He had not expected to sleep. Yet he must have dozed off as soon as his head touched the pillow. How could that be? He did not want to know. Again he felt sorry that there had been no raid on Beirut. The city had not faced real danger for far too long. Nerves had weakened in an excess of tranquility.

He switched on the radio. The announcer was only repeating the items Ramzy had heard the day before. He turned the dial to another station, which was talking about the fortitude of the Arab armies, their success in shooting down aircraft, and their advances into enemy territory.

NIMA ABDEL RAHIM jumped out of bed in their new house in Bayt Nuba. She looked at the clock. It was three-thirty in the morning. So she had not been awake, just dreaming that she was awake. She listened to the noise of the guns going off. Then she heard repeated knocks on their front door. She could hear her sister's voice from beneath the window.

Running over toward it, she called out, "Well, good morning!"

"What do you mean 'good'? The Israelis have entered the town."

Nima sped into her father's room. She woke him, telling him the news.

He shouted, "Impossible! Absolutely impossible! The Arab armies must have reached Jaffa by now. Just get back to bed."

Nima retreated to her room, but soon her sister was back, beating on the door. The whole village was in an uproar. Her father shouted that he wanted to know what was going on. Nima stared out of the window. People were running off into the fields. They were carrying bundles on their heads and not looking back. There were lights flashing everywhere, turning the night into day. The din was awful. The walls of the houses were shaking. An aircraft swept past overhead, fast and low. The noise almost made Nima lose her balance. Her mother kept insisting that they all get dressed. Her father was now wide awake and in a rage. Her little sister, Ayisha, was sobbing fearfully.

The mother went out, carrying a mattress, while the father carried Ayisha, and Nima carried clothing and bread. They ran together down the street. Little Ayisha reminded them that they had forgotten their pet lamb. The mother thought she ought to go back for it, but the father shouted that they keep on going. The entire population of Bayt Nuba was in flight together, heading out to the fields and caves. They were all under a spell. All they had left was the powerful drive to escape from death. All else was valueless. Nothing had meaning. Nima felt guilty about leaving the lamb; she could almost hear its bleating and feel its soft white wool against her face, and the brown patch on its face grew ever bigger before her eyes.

On the highway the people from Bayt Nuba met up with those from the villages of Amwas and Yalu. They, too, were under a spell. Deprived of all will, their only instinct was that of self-preservation. Lights flashed continually. There were explosions. The townspeople kept close to the ground and covered their heads with their arms.

THE PLANES kept flying over the houses of Jericho. They flashed through the air above the town with the speed of lightning, making a fearful noise. They swooped so low they almost touched the roofs and the tree tops. The very foundations of the houses shook. Windows shattered everywhere. All eyes were open wide in terror. Faces were pale and pinched, and some were bathed in sweat. People ran in all directions. Some took refuge in the orchards and in the surrounding fields.

The whole population of Jericho was spellbound. And so were the people from the big refugee camps near Jericho. All those items of value for which they had been living had lost their worth. The only thing they wanted now was to be safe. Self-preservation is the very finest of virtues. No one was truly awake. They were spread out on the ground, beneath the sky and the trees, turning their faces from the lights and blocking their ears against the explosions. The crying of the children tore their nerves to shreds and angered the frightened adults. They tried in vain to silence them, afraid the unseen enemy would discover their positions.

Taha Kanaan was still in the town hall trying to organize the people's resistance. He was composing a unit of volunteers for the defense of Jerusalem. He used the telephone to demand arms. It was impossible to get in touch with anyone. The telephone workers had all left. They had run away. He hated his countrymen. He tried to get in touch with his brother Issam in Jerusalem. Impossible. He rang his family. No reply. The thought that they had probably left the house and were hiding in the fields began to bother him. But he was sure his wife would know how to take care of everything. He had confidence in his daughter Adla, too. He thought of his son, Darwish, his only son. He was afraid for him. He busied himself in work. A bomb fell near the town hall. Glass cut someone's face.

KHALID ABDEL HALIM, in the village of Sabastia, took hold of his rifle. He wanted to join the popular resistance. His mother got up and stood in his way. He made no reply to her, just stared at her angrily. His anger increased when she reminded him that he was the only member of the family who could be counted on. He hustled her out of his way without saying a word. She hung onto him, screaming, "And who's going to care for your wife, your daughter, your sister Khayriya and her son, and your other sister's children?"

His anger flamed at her stubborn refusal, even at this time, to refer to his other sister by name. He shouted at her, as he had so often longed to do before, "Say 'your sister Fada.' Mention her name! You're the cause! You forced her to marry an old man, then talked my brother into killing her!"

"She disgraced the family!"

"Disgraced the family! Because she ran away from an old man you had forced on her?"

"Be silent!"

"And you are the one who's responsible for Khayriya's marriage."

"Keep quiet!"

He did not want to be silent. He wanted to put an end to her. She treated them just like the other things she owned. And she did this in the name of her concern for their interests and her love for them.

He pulled free of her and ran to the door. She continued reciting the names of all the family members dependent on him. But she made no mention of herself. She always pretended not to care for herself and that all she was looking out for was the good of the family.

He shot out of the house, slamming the door behind

him, and hurried toward the main square. There was no one there. He found some of his friends; they conferred together, tried to organize themselves, but failed. There were not enough weapons. They cursed the Arab governments.

Khalid returned home, broken. He could not go inside. He sat on a rock in front of the door. There was no target at which to aim his gun.

AZMY ABDEL QADIR had not slept that night. He searched the streets of old Jerusalem for the enemy, his hand gripping his machine gun. He strained his ears at every noise. This war was getting on his nerves much more than the war of 1948 had. Everything was happening so fast. There was no real confrontation. The enemy was relying on aircraft. From time to time the aircraft would drop flares that turned night into day. There were explosions and the sound of buildings collapsing. If only he could see the enemy's face! He kept his gun at the ready. He was not going to remain "innocent" as he had in 1948. Then he had given refuge to a German-Jewish doctor and his family in his own home. The son of that doctor might very well be a pilot blasting the houses of Jerusalem.

RAMZY DESPAIRED of listening to the Arab broadcasting stations. He tuned in a Western station. They were talking as if the war were already over. He did not want to believe it.

He left his apartment. He had to talk to someone. When it occurred to him that he had left without shaving, he ridiculed his own inanity and continued quickly on toward the university. He had not consciously intended to go there but merely found himself heading in that direction. Perhaps he wanted to know what the professors and students were doing. When he was with them he always had a sense of hope and confidence in the Arab world and in himself, despite the lack of optimism that characterized their talk—or perhaps because of this lack of optimism. At least they were not totally duped.

It pained him that the Arab universities were isolated and living in either the past or the future. It had become accepted that students not participate in the present. They were being trained to believe that students must prepare for the future by attending lectures, studying, learning, and developing their potential. Ramzy himself could not understand how students could study, learn, and develop their potential without actual participation. He could not see culture in isolation but only in participation. Yet the universities, both in their own view and in that of most Arabs and Arab governments, were an ideal place, divorced from life itself.

But Ramzy did delight in his colleagues and students. They were idealistic and understanding at times of crisis. It hurt him that with their tremendous potential they were disorganized and thwarted. He did not know of one colleague or student who was active on behalf of his country at its darkest hour. Hundreds of teachers and thousands of students were, just like the rest of the people, reading newspapers, listening to the radio, watching television, or merely shouting. That was all. His friend Salah Said, a pilot living in exile, was now no doubt burning angrily, like dry straw. He was to have arrived at the border the day before. Would they accept his services or put him in jail? Ramzy's friend Amin Badr, a radar expert also living in exile, was working in France for a big company which considered him one of its most important employees.

47

Ramzy could just imagine him now, pacing his room in Paris like a tiger in a circus cage. Another friend, Izzedin, with a doctorate in engineering, must be leaving his laboratory at the University of California and feeling cut off and disoriented. His friend Khalid, a chemical engineer, must be fidgeting in front of a television set in Cleveland, Ohio. Other friends of his at universities all over the United States must be longing for contact with their roots. They must all be livid with rage, scarcely able to stand the insults directed at the Arabs in the newspapers and magazines and on television and radio, and confused by all the bias against the Arabs. Why all the hatred? Why all this new anti-Semitism?

Ramzy felt as if his country were a dismembered body. The eyes were disconnected from the face. The arms were disjointed from the torso. The brains were all drained. The feet ruled over things.

The students' loudspeakers were still blaring news, patriotic songs, and speeches. The crowd had been there since early morning, listening, discussing, and cheering. Ramzy chatted with several of his students, all wanting to know what they could do to help. Many suggestions were made, but were disregarded as impractical. One student, Basim, was burning with such enthusiasm that he could not keep his thoughts to any one topic. He was in a nervous state of constant movement and deliberately avoided mixing with the rest. His hope of returning to Acre, although fading, was not entirely gone. He pursued avidly any news hinting of an Arab victory, no matter how insignificant the battle. Basim seemed under a mental siege. Threatened and exposed to his very roots, he was searching for some means of escape. At the same time he was curled up within himself, like a hedgehog in danger; he felt incohesive, like sand. His various parts repelled one another, as if they did not belong to him.

A second student, Ghaith, desperately wanted to do something and kept insisting on the need for organization. Despite everything, he was maintaining his sense of humor and keenness of perception. He was from a small, isolated village in the Koura region of northern Lebanon, but obviously felt himself to be a stone from the walls of Jerusalem.

Two of the women students in the group, Nahida and Nuha, had not previously concerned themselves with politics. They had restricted their activities to studying and party-going. May, on the other hand, was conservative politically, but radical socially. She hated the word *socialism* and ridiculed the "revolutionary" movements; she loved to tell dirty jokes about their leaders. She also liked to discuss sex.

Another student, Nasib, was from a prominent family that accepted unquestioningly whatever was exported from the West; he rarely showed any interest in politics. Latif was a medical student, a person difficult to understand. He was rather withdrawn and expressed his true feelings only among his closest friends. Salma had an active and inquisitive temperament. She loved people, just as she did sports and engaging in social welfare work. Absolutely nothing could keep her away from other people. She disliked both books and school. Her only interest was in people.

Siham, the last in the group, seemed to be deeply affected by the war; she was forgetting her personal problems. Recently she had often come to Ramzy's office to get counseling from him as her faculty adviser. She was in love with a student whom she did not respect and wanted to understand why she loved him. She considered him unattractive, unintelligent, superficial, and, in short, contemptible. It infuriated her that he took so little interest in her, his disinterest seeming to increase the closer she tried to get. And the greater his disinterest, the more she felt she could not study, eat, or sleep without seeing him. She felt somehow that he possessed her and that she was powerless before him. But it seemed that the war had made her forget her problem. She was thinking about her family in Jerusalem and avidly following all the news.

The whole group was eventually assembled in Ramzy's office.

Nahida asked, "Well, then, what have we decided to do?"

"That's a subject still bothering me," Ramzy said.

"We're ready to do anything that you suggest," said Ghaith.

"Why don't we offer our services to the state?" suggested Nasib.

"But I don't think Lebanon has any need for us," Basim objected.

"Lebanon is safe. Nothing's going to happen here," said Salma.

"If only we were in Jerusalem," sighed Ghaith.

Siham turned her head and drew away from the rest. She was thinking of her family; her heart was pounding. She could imagine a bomb dropping on their house, turning it into a grave enclosing her father, mother, brother, and sister. She would be left alone, like a single island in the vastness of the ocean, rain falling only on her. Why had these images sprung to her mind? Her family was probably fine. Things seemed worse from a distance. Nothing would happen to her family.

Salma sat down beside Siham. Ghaith was getting ready

to leave. Basim had not completely abandoned hope of a victory for the Arabs and so was not particularly concerned for his family in Nablus. Latif, however, was worried about his family in Ramallah, close to Jerusalem.

RAMZY DID NOT REALLY KNOW how he felt; hope and despair were still battling for control within him. There were many signs now that the Arabs were going to lose the war; but he, too, grasped at any straw of news suggesting an Arab success, constantly repeating it to himself and to others. He was delighted when it was reported that Egypt would today move into the attack, and that battle was still raging in Jerusalem. He cheered along with the rest when it was announced from the Arab capitals that 176 Israeli planes had been shot down.

"It seems there's some encouraging news. What is it?"

It was Pamela's voice. Ramzy turned and answered her in English that the Arabs had shot down 176 planes.

"Really?" she asked.

"Well, I don't know what's real and what isn't any more."

"It's not important whether the news is correct or false."

"Then what is important? What do you mean?"

"What would be important would be to hear that Israel had shot down Arab planes."

"What are you driving at?"

"Don't get annoyed! It seems you don't understand. I mean—you know what I mean! What would you think if you heard that Israel had downed Arab planes?"

"What would you have me think?"

"Oh dear! What has come over you? That would mean that the Arabs were attacking."

"You are right. That's what scares me."

It occurred to him that she should have left Lebanon. Yesterday he had heard that the American embassy was urging its citizens to leave.

Gazing at her golden hair, he said: "So you haven't left yet!"

"Why should I leave?"

"I don't know."

"Do you want me to leave?"

Her question embarrassed him. It seemed she knew how he felt about her.

Haltingly, he replied: "It's not for me to decide—"

"I don't think I'm going to leave."

"But the embassy wants you to."

"I don't allow anyone to tell me what I ought to do. You know that," she asserted, referring to what he knew of her relationship to her husband.

"I do know that you reject any authority over you," he agreed, "but don't you think Walter needs you and would like you to join him?"

"Don't forget that Walter is my husband and that marriage represents authority. And anyway, I no longer feel that he really is my husband."

"Are you sure about that?"

Ramzy was glad she had not left. But he did not want her to know how he felt. Not yet, at any rate. They both were silent. She was apparently deep in thought, uncertain, or perhaps wondering if Ramzy was really dense.

Their silence was broken by sounds of cheers mixed with laughter at a news item just announced over the loudspeakers.

Ramzy turned to a student and asked him in Arabic, "What's the news? What is it?"

"Yemen has declared war on Israel!"

They exchanged grins. He turned to Pamela and found

her looking at him expectantly, waiting to hear what had happened. He hesitated but said, "Yemen has declared war on Israel."

"Oh! That's important news! Now you're going to win the war!"

He said nothing. His country was a mass of wounds within his heart. His country was piles of rubble. He was part of one of those heaps. It was as though he were a pile of stones heaped together: earthquakes were occurring deep inside himself; the rocks were crumbling, falling, and scattering. Never before had he felt so powerless. He had no control over his destiny. He had no solid core. He was a jumble of parts fighting with one another instead of taking form together.

He thought of going to his office, but did not really want to. If only he could be alone to contemplate and to wallow in his own misery. But perhaps he was being overly pessimistic. Who could tell? The Arabs might win the battle after all. What the Western news stations were saying might well be an attempt to demoralize the Arabs. The Arab broadcasts were still talking of battles raging in Jerusalem, the Negev, Gaza, and Jenin. Syria was still referring to its advances inside Israel and its destruction of the settlements near Lake Huleh.

The loudspeakers were announcing another important news item. Everyone listened in silence: "Cairo and Amman are charging the United States and Britain with giving assistance to Israel!"

Ramzy was shocked, even though he had no doubts about the pro-Israel bias of the two countries. The students' angry shouts were reverberating everywhere. He explained to Pamela what had happened. She, too, was dumbfounded.

"It's not possible. It's impossible," she said. But then

she corrected herself, "No, it is possible. The United States is insane. What it's doing in the Middle East is no different from what it's doing in Viet Nam."

The uproar was increasing. The students were running in all directions. It seemed they were going to try to do something.

One of them shouted, "Let's go to the American embassy, everybody!"

"To the American embassy," shouted another voice.

And so the furious students began massing.

Pamela asked him, "Are you going to take part in the demonstration?"

"No."

"Why not? I think you ought to participate."

"And you, are you going to take part?"

"Why, of course."

"Why?"

"The American government has become a tool of the industrialists and the militarists. It's as much against the American people as it is against the Vietnamese and the Arabs."

"I don't want to dampen your enthusiasm. I just want to understand."

"You're not taking part?"

"I don't think so."

"Where are you going then?"

"To my office."

"Will you wait for me there?"

"Yes, I will."

"Be sure you do. I have to see you."

It seemed she really did have something to say to him. He asked, "Why is that?"

"Oh, I just have to see you. That's all."

"Well, what's your problem?"

"Problem? There's no problem. It's a very simple matter. Come on! You know, sometimes you really are a disappointment."

She could sense that he was truly confused. She remained silent for a moment or two and then added, "Kathy has turned in the key to her flat and left, so I have nowhere to sleep tonight. Perhaps you can help me find a hotel which won't cost more than a couple of dollars a day."

"Oh, that's easy. I'll be waiting for you—" He laughed as he said that. But he could feel she did not appreciate the joke. He knew that she could not afford even two dollars. In Europe she and her husband had been sleeping in the parks.

Ramzy wondered, as he watched her join the crowds of students, why it had to happen now, in the middle of a war. He felt like a hunter without a gun, whose prey stood calmly gazing at him. If Kathy had left earlier, he would have invited Pamela to stay in his apartment. So why not invite her now? He would invite her. But he'd be in no mood to flirt with her.

All of a sudden the dams broke, and the quiet, stagnant waters, built up for ages past, were transformed into a foaming, roaring flood tide, sweeping away everything in its path. The students streamed off toward the American embassy, carrying all the rocks, stones, and pebbles in their path. Their faces, their voices, and their eyes had somehow changed.

The flood arrived at the embassy. Stones flew through the air. Glass broke. Groups of demonstrators from the other schools and universities of Beirut were arriving. Cars were aflame. Some people were trying to get inside the embassy. A rapid succession of gunshots was heard, and this increased the anger. A unit of the public security forces and the army was assembling. Someone said that the embassy officials were shooting, and even more stones were flung at the windows. A number of other cars were in flames. A student collapsed, wounded, and the students raced over and picked him up. Blood was streaming from his shoulder. Shouts increased in anger. Bullets reverberated. Flames swept upward. Other waves of students were approaching. Another detachment of the army was coming, too. Streams of people who were not students were arriving from all directions. Everyone was shouting, screaming, and hurling insults and slogans while they threw stones and burned cars. The air was filled with rocks. More people were injured. More anger. More terror, more running, more throwing. Most of the windows had been broken. Most of the cars were burning.

Someone let out the shout: "On to the British embassy, everyone! To the British embassy!"

Someone else took up the cry: "The British embassy!"

More joined in the same shout. The floods of demonstrators moved on to their new goal, arming themselves with more stones and sticks and chunks of wood. Other demonstrators were already there. Streams of stones flew toward the windows. Shots reverberated. More people fell, wounded. Sirens wailed, their shrieking noise penetrating to the very entrails. A number of wounded students were shoved in the ambulances. The shrieking was resumed. Then the ambulances disappeared, their noise subsiding, leaving behind the sound of glass breaking and the din from bullets, songs, and shouts. More soldiers were arriving, too, in trucks and in armored cars. Everyone was retreating. Soon the campus was swarming with students again.

Then the order to clear the university was issued, and soon everything was quiet. The shouting was transformed into a deep, inaudible panting; a mystic unification was attained, and total calm prevailed. A sad wind moved through the trees, leaves, and flowers of the campus. The falling leaves mixed with the dust and debris left by the students.

A sad calm enveloped Ramzy. He felt as if he, too, were left prostrate like the leaves, abandoned on the ground. The breeze blew him wherever it wished. He was powerless to resist. He did not even try. His sadness approached sheer despair. He had no control over his world, no control over his country, no control over himself. It was the wind that controlled him. Here, in June, it was turning into an autumn day. The very quiet was forlorn. He could not believe what had happened to his country. Jerusalem was burning. Palestine was turning into ruin, like Sodom. Nothing in it seemed able to withstand the conflagration. But he looked back at his country, back at the past. He did not care if he were to turn into a pillar of salt.

ALY ABDEL RAHIM looked back. He pretended to be looking at his wife and two daughters, Nima and Ayisha, but he was gazing at the village of Bayt Nuba. The mother was again carrying the mattress on her head, while Nima gripped Ayisha by the hand. They had joined the rest of the people from Bayt Nuba and those from Yalu and Amwas in the orchards and caves, hoping that the fighting would cease and that they could return to their homes. Suddenly they were aware that the enemy was drawing near. There were explosions and the reverberations of guns, the whining of bullets, the noise of fires, trees falling, the fronts of some caves tumbling down, children crying, women wailing. There was no chance for resistance. Instead of returning home, they were picking up their packs and moving off toward Bayt Awr. They would wait there until the battle ended. There was grief in their eyes.

AZMY ABDEL QADIR ran toward his house, near the walls of old Jerusalem. Someone had told him that his neighborhood had been bombed and that fire was consuming the grass and trees and the wood of the windows and doors. He stopped dead when he saw his house. It had been transformed into a heap of stones. His neighbors were picking through the rubble. He ran. He searched feverishly for his family beneath the debris.

Many families were streaming past the spot on their way out of Jerusalem. He paid no attention. The number of neighbors helping him was dwindling; they continued digging.

A woman screamed. She had seen an arm amid all the stones and dirt. She was wailing now, striking herself in the face in lamentation. They quickly dug around the arm.

A plane dived toward them and they threw themselves down in the rubble. It flew off and then was back, shooting at them time after time. One of Azmy's neighbors suffered a minor wound, but he wanted no help for himself. They continued digging around the arm. Azmy was sure now that it was the arm of his little son, Husny. He dug feverishly and at last pulled him out. He could not look at his knee, which was open with the bone sticking out. One of the neighbors took the boy from him, to be carried to the hospital and to the care of Sister Marie Thérèse and Father Paul.

Azmy continued digging in the debris for his wife and three remaining children. Sister Marie Thérèse had arrived now and began to help. Suddenly Azmy's hand struck the foot of one of his children, and he stopped for a moment. Then he got down on his knees and began to dig frantically. He lifted the pieces of wood and stone. Then he closed his eyes tightly. His wife was stretched out, motionless, still clutching three of her children. He leaped forward, groveling close to them. He sobbed once and then continued sobbing rapidly. He could control himself no longer.

Sister Marie Thérèse called for her assistant and asked some of the men to help him in placing the bodies in the cart exactly as they were, with the mother still hugging her three children. She kept hold of Azmy. He placed his face between her hands and wept. His tears burned her palms. She remembered her experiences in the Second World War, when she had worked in a hospital on the Swiss border. The face of a Jew who had lost his children came back to her mind. Her own eyes were watering now, try as she could to stop them. She said a prayer to Jesus, beseeching him to extend to Azmy Abdel Qadir the strength to go on living.

RAMZY'S COLLEAGUES Bashir, Nadir, and Kamil came into his study and listened with him to the transistor radio. Standing with his hands in his pockets, Kamil said nervously: "I believe the war is over. The entire Egyptian air force was destroyed before it ever left the ground."

Nadir objected, "But that just doesn't make sense."

"How can you explain, then, the failure of the Egyptian air force to take part in the battle?"

Nadir answered coldly, "Well, it may be a matter of military strategy. The Egyptian army may be using the plan the Russians used with both Napoleon and Hitler."

Kamil smiled scornfully. "That's no explanation—just wishful thinking."

Ramzy thought it best to change the subject, so he asked, "Well, do you all think there'd be any sense in the United States aiding Israel in such an obvious manner?"

"I don't believe so," Kamil replied.

"Well, I don't discount the possibility so long as there's a quick-on-the-draw cowboy in charge of the American government."

"What bothers me," commented Bashir, joining the discussion, "is that we are a people who have lost both their identity and their sense of manhood. Each one of us is suffering from a split personality, especially in Lebanon. We are Arab, and yet our education is in some cases French, in some cases Anglo-Saxon, and in others Eastern-Mystic. A very strange mixture. We're all schizophrenic. We need to go back and search out our roots. That's why I get enthusiastic at what the blacks in America are saying about Black Power."

Ramzy suggested they listen to the news broadcast. The announcer stated that Jordanian artillery was still shelling Tel Aviv, and that Israel feared an Arab attack on the road leading down to Qalqilya and to Tel Aviv. They traced the area on a map of Palestine.

Bashir asked, "How far is it?"

"Twelve kilometers from the border to Tel Aviv," answered Nadir. "There's probably an Arab advance from Tulkarm toward Natanya. With that they would cut Israel in two."

"And Lebanon would occupy the northern portion," Ramzy commented sarcastically.

Nadir recited a line of modern Arabic poetry: "A battle cry surges in my blood;/determination breathes in my lungs."

HIS VISITORS gone, Ramzy remained in his office alone. Silence. He stared at the map of Palestine. He put his hands inside his pockets as if searching for something. He went over to the window. There was a breeze moving the leaves and the dust. He went back and sat down. What was he to do? Where could he go? He got up once more. He simply could not remain alone. Paradise without other people would be a hell. Earth was in fact paradise, purgatory, and hell. There were no heavens. Purgatory and hell alone were reality. And paradise was just a dream thought up by man to fulfill those desires he could not achieve in reality.

It occurred to him that he was a pessimist, gloomy, alienated, and cynical, especially about himself. Why did he let himself get so carried away by events of the moment? He could not answer that question. Reality was neither paradise nor hell, but purgatory. Paradise was a world without disappointment or crisis; hell, a world without hope. Both were imaginary. The real world was purgatory. He repeated the idea to himself. The world was a series of trials and disappointments, but it was also always in motion toward some hope or other. Despair and hope had the same face and yet were in eternal conflict. But it was disappointment that was living deep inside both him and his people these days. This would not last long. It could not and must not last long.

He glanced at his watch; it was two o'clock. He ought

to have lunch. He had not even had breakfast. But he was still not hungry. He sat down in an armchair, letting his thoughts wander.

Pamela came in. He had forgotten that he had promised to wait for her and was glad he had not left earlier. Her arrival was like a light giving off warmth and clearing the gloom. He stared at her long blond hair. She noticed that he was looking at her and turned as though to ask why he was staring in that way.

"What about going for a walk?" he suggested.

"Where?"

"Not outside the university, of course."

"Why not? Is there any danger there?"

"It's dangerous to go out with you under normal circumstances."

She smiled but said nothing. It was better like that. She would pretend not to understand what he was getting at. But was she, anyway, interested in what he was implying? Surely she did not want to begin a new love affair. It was time she settled down. Was he the man she could love and settle down with?

Ramzy was thinking how much he liked her hair and her tall, slim figure. There was strength and determination in her face, too. Yet she did seem somehow bewildered as well. Perhaps she was feeling guilty. She was often silent, and he longed to know what she was thinking. But she talked freely whenever they discussed a philosophical subject. She became a new person.

They walked off together onto the campus. Neither spoke for some while. There were many questions he would have liked to ask her. Her whole position there was very odd. He could not understand why she refused to leave like the rest of the Americans. Most of them had gone, all except a few who had fled to villages in the mountains or who had stayed inside their houses. Was she just an adventurous type? He remembered she had talked much about Hemingway. Or perhaps she was a spy. She certainly had no business being in the Middle East. She was a "tourist," yet one who never left. For all she knew, the war might last a long time. And he could not understand how she had allowed her sick husband to return alone to America. She was a strange woman. They had been living with her friend Kathy, who had now left. So where would she stay? Should he take her to his apartment? No, he couldn't do that. What would his neighbors and friends say? What would Najla say if she heard? And what about Fatina? Actually, he wasn't sure that he loved Najla anymore; and he had no interest in Fatina. No, the really important objection was that while his country was in a state of war, he would be inviting a young married woman to stay in his apartment. It just was not right. But he could not send her off to some cheap hotel. He was a man, after all. What was he afraid of anyway? If she was not scared, why should he be? He was still too conservative. But what if she were a spy? Well, if she were, she would not have picked him. What could he tell her? What information could she possibly get from him?

He must have been smiling to himself as these thoughts crossed his mind.

She asked him, "Well, what are you smiling at?"

"Nothing. Nothing at all."

Her question took him by surprise. He had concluded that she was just adventurous, that was all.

She repeated her question. "No, why are you smiling?"

"It's nothing, really nothing," he pretended once more.

He told himself again that she was just adventurous, that she loved to travel and wanted to get to know the world, that she was like so many young Americans who doubted that their impressions of the world outside were true ones. Their desire to see the world in its reality was increased by their lack of faith in their newspapers and magazines and in their government. The news was distorted. They wanted to know the facts as they were.

His silence was annoying her now. She wondered what to say. What could he be thinking? He seemed preoccupied. This confusion of his must mean she had begun to have an impact on him. She was pleased at this deduction. Let him stay confused.

Pamela had told him that she and Walter had worked for five years to save the money to travel round the world. They had lived in Europe for a while before coming to Lebanon. They were both artists, and the paintings they had made throughout their trip differed remarkably from country to country, in both color and form.

Pamela and Walter often had serious arguments. Her friend Kathy had told Ramzy that they shouted at one another constantly and even came to blows; sometimes their fighting lasted into the night. According to Kathy, they argued because Pamela was self-reliant whereas Walter depended on others, and because she liked to display her charms, something he disliked. Or perhaps she liked to flirt precisely because she did not get along with him. Pamela had herself told Ramzy that she and Walter fought a great deal. She said he was very jealous and conservative despite his outwardly free life-style. Actually, she did not care if he did feel jealous. What annoyed her most was his dependence on her. And he was always complaining of his "illness." He would describe his pains and feelings over and over, thousands of times, in the same words and manner. And he was always saying that he would not be able to go on living without her. He wanted her to remain near him.

She had gone out with Ramzy on a number of occasions. Her appearance and behavior seemed to imply that she wanted to flirt, but she would clam up whenever he broached a nonphilosophical subject, making him feel that they were worlds apart. Her eyes did light up whenever he mentioned anything intellectual, especially painting, poetry, or fiction. She did a great deal of reading as well as painting and liked to record her feelings, thoughts, and experiences in words and pictures. Her diary was full of words, colors, and drawings. One exciting discovery she had made was that Arabs draw with the letters of their alphabet. She had tried to make strange shapes and forms out of the Latin letters. The results had disappointed her, however, so she had begun learning Arabic.

Ramzy remembered how they had played tennis together and had gone swimming together, how they had discussed literature and authors and the alienation of young Americans. They had flirted in the sea and on the beach, and had looked for pretty pebbles. One day they had walked up the Dog River Valley, a few miles outside Beirut, and had traced it to its hilly source. Ramzy recalled how delighted Pamela had been at the diversity and beauty of the wildflowers they had seen and how eagerly she had collected some.

Pamela had not let him hold her hand as they climbed over the rocks, and he had felt confused. Could she be interested in him? Sometimes she seemed to consider him just a good friend. She was probably using him. She needed someone to accompany her and to take her about in a car. Yet other times she did seem attached to him and told him how happy she felt when talking to him.

At one particularly steep rock face, he had found his body close to hers, his face near her face; he had felt the warmth of her breath, as she must have felt his. But she had suggested they continue their walk, and he had at once struck up a conversation about her paintings.

Now, as they strolled through the campus, Ramzy asked her, "Do you believe Walter will continue writing to you?"

"He'll write every day and say that the doctors have discovered he has a serious illness and so he was not imagining things. He'll want me to go back to him, or at least to feel guilty for not going back to him."

"What else will he tell you?"

"He'll say he needs me more and more, that he weeps like a child, and that he's all alone in the heart of New York City. He'll criticize me for not returning with him, and he'll ask me whether I'm moving from one Arab to another."

"He has friends?"

"Oh yes, many. They often get together for parties. But he'll tell me that these parties only increase his sense of loneliness. Each of his friends will be accompanied by his wife or girlfriend."

"I can well understand that."

"Sometimes I do feel guilty. But at the same time I feel that there is a great psychological gulf separating me from him when he behaves like that. I feel he's behaving like a child. He's very dependent on me. When we're together I just don't feel free. Even when I read his letters I don't feel free. The only time I really felt I loved him was when he would stand on his own two feet and act independently, even act against my will. I want to feel I'm his wife and his friend, not his mother."

Ramzy laughed, but Pamela continued without laughing:

"When he wants something from me he tries to get my sympathy, to make me feel sorry for him. Do you know how he tried to persuade me to return with him?"

"How?"

"He would tell me he could sense death approaching and that he would hate to die alone. These attempts at arousing my pity just made me more determined not to return. I just couldn't help feeling that way."

Ramzy wondered if she was telling him all this to attract him. Despite all his doubts they were soon in his car heading for his apartment. The first thing he did when they arrived was to turn on the radio. The announcer began with a news summary.

"Fierce battles are raging near Jenin. The Jordanians are fighting heroically."

"Advances are being made on all fronts by Egyptian, Syrian, Jordanian, and Iraqi forces."

"Egypt has closed the Suez Canal."

"Iraq and Kuwait have stopped pumping oil."

"The Soviet Union has deplored the aggression."

"Hand-to-hand combat continues in Jerusalem."

"Merchants profiteering in foodstuffs have been jailed."

He turned to another station, which was broadcasting rousing military music, music that in fact failed to arouse his spirits. It merely seemed ludicrous to him.

He switched off the radio. Pamela was taking a shower. He thought he would listen to Wagner's *Flying Dutchman*.

Once more Palestine, like the *Flying Dutchman*, had been given the opportunity to reach its goal. But now it seemed that the goal was receding and that Palestine might have to return to the sea once more, to live amid the waves, with no hope of death or life. The *Flying Dutchman* was returning to the sea. The captain had not found a woman who would love him till death. The sea had thrown him ashore but would now receive him back. There was no way out into life for him.

Ramzy hated the thought of spending his life before a map of Palestine, conjuring up images of its orchards and beaches. He wanted to be inside it and a part of it, to live on its soil. He wanted to hear the sound of its waves, savor the fragrance of its citrus groves.

But the song that was echoing in his mind was only creating false hope. The gods would prevent his return. The gods did not want him to live happily in peace, at home. The gods did not desire peace for those who did not submit to their will. The gods did not like men to be free and independent. They liked them devoid of personal pride. One's duty was to listen and submit, without understanding why.

One was told that the wisdom of the gods was far beyond human comprehension, and that man therefore had to be submissive. Ramzy was pleased to understand all that, yet it pained him that he could not overcome the gods.

But he might strike some target. Radiance would return to his face when doubt in Palestine ended, and when its doubt in him ended. Or the radiance might return to his face when he was true to Palestine. Or when Palestine was true to his honor and freedom. But he was not true to Palestine, nor was it true to his honor and freedom, both of which it ignored or treated with disdain. When would he find Palestine? When would Palestine discover him? He was lost, and his country was astray. The son lost, the father lost. How long would he journey aimlessly?

Resoluteness would be his only goal. He was not stubborn; it was just that he knew the value of freedom. To announce that he would not submit to the status quo was blasphemy in the eyes of the gods, and they would be angry when they heard that. They would swear to cast him out on the seas forever, and he would wander without victory or peace. And Palestine would remain accursed as long as it refused to seek the gods' forgiveness or give up its love for freedom.

Ramzy's craving for his land would give him no peace. It was both a madness and a love song. Perhaps he was still a child, not knowing what his love song meant, only knowing that he could not live at peace with himself without a song to sing. He wondered if he was to view his country from afar forever? He was sure that he would never return to it until he gave it himself and was true to it till death.

For that reason Ramzy listened for news of guerrilla activities more eagerly than for news of Arab regular army activities, even though he did so unconsciously. The guerrilla was, to him, the best example of someone with a life-long commitment. Like all the rest, Ramzy was concerned with petty matters—family, possessions, and work. He was enslaved by his desire to own a car and a house, infatuated with restaurants, cafés, and clubs. He was addicted to so many pleasures, unable to give them up by simple rejection or the exercise of self-control. In contrast to himself, a guerrilla was a person who could resist any temptation and remain true to something till death.

AZMY ABDEL QADIR went into the hospital. They gave him something to eat and drink, but he could only drink. Other men were there, taking refuge, handing over their weapons, and dressing in nurses' overalls. The Israeli soldiers might enter at any time.

Father Paul said to Azmy, "If you want to remain here, you must hand over the machine gun. If the Israelis come here and find it on you, they will blow up the hospital."

"I know that. I will leave."

Azmy was now accustomed to the noise of gunfire and bombing, the shells and the explosions, and to the sight of the wounded and the dying in the streets.

ISSAM KANAAN, horrified at what was happening in Jerusalem, had left with his family for Jericho, where his brother Taha lived. There was no hope now for an Arab victory, so why expose his children to death? No one would blame him for leaving. He couldn't delay either; the longer he waited the more the transportation charges would be. The drivers were no longer talking shillings and pence; it was all pounds now.

On the road to Jericho they avoided the aircraft as best they could. A plane bombed one bus ahead of them. They shivered with fright as the bus burst into flames. Some people managed to escape. One man emerged with flames covering his body. As he ran, the flames only increased. Issam shouted for him to roll on the ground. The plane was coming back again, and this time it hit the bus that had been carrying them. He was relieved he had got his family out in time. They continued their journey on foot. Now he realized he had brought his family out of Jerusalem only to expose them to danger of death on the road. If only he had done like some other families and taken refuge in the mosques, hospitals, churches, and monasteries! But all he could do now was complete the journey to Jericho.

ABU RIZK and his wife decided to leave. They took their children, a mattress, and a bundle of clothes, and wandered off, with no idea where to go.

KHALID ABDEL HALIM was leaving Sabastia, too. Once again his mother was having her way; his wife and sister had both sided with her. She was now leading the family away, carrying a large pack on her head. Khalid carried his daughter, Manwa, and another suitcase. His wife, Arabiya, was carrying a mattress, even though she was eight months pregnant. His sister Khayriya was carrying her son, Tariq, and a basket of clothes. They were heading for the mountains, avoiding the main roads. They all were afraid. A long time would pass before they would look once more over the Jordan Valley. The explosions told them that the enemy was nearing Nablus.

THE PEOPLE of Neby Samwil, now in the caves, learned that the enemy had occupied their village.

An elder, Sheikh Muhy al-Din, addressed them: "We must not run away. I believe it will be best if we return to our homes. Israeli rule can be no worse than British or Turkish rule. We endured Turkish rule and British rule. They both faded away, but we remained. Israeli rule must surely fade too, but we will remain."

The people of Neby Samwil accepted the elder's suggestion readily and went back to the village, but they were amazed at what they found there. Their houses had been plundered. Some were in ruins. No matter. They would endure it all. They would begin again. But they soon realized that they would have to begin their lives in a new place, for the soldiers chased them out of their homes, saying that their village had become a military zone and that they could not be permitted to remain there.

The people plodded wearily off toward Bir Nabala. Mahmud Kamil and his wife and nine children took refuge in a deserted house. They would try to sleep without food.

ABDULLAH ISMAIL in Hebron feared for his thirteen children and two wives. People were saying that the Israelis had manufactured huge daggers, with blades as long as a forearm, which they called "Hebron knives." They wanted vengeance for the 1929 massacre. Many of the people in Hebron were terrified that the Israelis would take revenge on them. Abdullah cursed the British, who had engineered the massacre. His father had told him that it was a British officer, wanting to stir up trouble between the Arabs and the Jews, who had released some Arab prisoners and incited them to do away with the Jews.

Abdullah hated to run away. He was not afraid for himself, but for his children, who were more precious to him than anything else in the world. His first wife had not borne him children. He had waited for her to do so for twelve years. He had loved her and had not wanted to divorce her. So he had decided to marry a second woman. He had discussed it all with his first wife. She had reluctantly agreed to the plan; actually, she had been quite satisfied because it meant no divorce. The second wife became pregnant immediately. And then an incredible surprise—a month later the first wife became pregnant. No one could understand it. They said it must be jealousy! So the years had passed with the second wife producing six children and the first, seven.

Abdullah decided to leave before the Israelis arrived with their "Hebron knives."

RAMZY SENSED Pamela standing over him as he stretched out in the armchair. He stared up at her. She had wrapped a long bath towel around her tall, slim figure. He pretended not to notice and looked at the glass of whiskey in her hand.

Pamela kissed him on the ear and said, "You know, we free souls don't conform to the values and institutions controlling society."

"Why don't you conform?"

"The values are not consistent with one another. They are contradictory. People are hypocrites, especially the value-arbiters and the higher-ups in the power-structure. Their conduct does not conform to their beliefs. The institutions are designed to transform us into machines. They rob us of our freedom and try to make us all alike—weak, submissive, obedient creatures. Life in America is just a rat race—a race with no real meaning for the competitors. The important thing is to run. The important thing is success.

"Once, after taking LSD, I felt that I had fused with the river of life within me, and that I had followed it back to its source. All colors changed—they glowed and radiated. And sounds changed, too. I could hear the throbbing of my blood through my veins. I could hear every movement I made. My vision changed. I could almost see the atoms of my own brain. My perception became acute, and I noticed things I had never noticed before. We accept the existence of many things without examining them closely. There is so much that doesn't arouse the slightest curiosity in us. But with LSD each object awakens

some sort of curiosity in you. You discover new relationships between things. Your mood changes also. I would
switch with fantastic speed between laughing and crying."

How brave she was, Ramzy thought as she stopped and
looked at the records, rapidly rubbing her hair dry. If
only he had her courage! He didn't even have the courage
to travel alone, afraid that he would not rest properly.
But she insisted on traveling on and on, even without
the means to ensure the simplest forms of food, clothing,
and accommodation. She never cared what people said
about her. He cared a great deal about such things. He
thought that her remarks about hypocrites had been
directed at him. He had told her he was concerned that
she had allowed her sick husband to return alone, but
at the same time he was pleased she had remained on
her own. Perhaps they could now become friends—even
lovers.

She selected a recording of T. S. Eliot's poetry. "May
I listen to this?"

"Of course."

They listened to Eliot recite "The Love Song of J. Alfred
Prufrock." She sat in the armchair facing his. From time
to time she repeated phrases along with Eliot and sometimes preceded him.

In the room the women come and go
Talking of Michelangelo.

There was a pause and then she repeated along with
Eliot:

. . . "Do I dare?" and, "Do I dare?"
. . . Do I dare
  Disturb the universe?

Another pause. Eliot's voice had a strange echoing quality. Pamela straightened her posture in the chair as Eliot continued:

I have measured out my life with coffee spoons.

She moved to sit close to Ramzy when she heard the poet recite:

Should I, after tea and cakes and ices,
Have the strength to force the moment to its crisis?

Ramzy let her snuggle up close to him. He stroked her hair and recited with Eliot:

I am no prophet . . .
. . . No! I am not Prince Hamlet, nor was meant to be;
. . . Advise the prince; no doubt, an easy tool,
. . . Politic, cautious, and meticulous.

Pamela smiled and asked him why he did not join in where the poet reached the line:

I grow old . . .

Ramzy laughed loudly when Eliot pondered:

. . . Do I dare to eat a peach?

She laughed too, and Ramzy felt slightly annoyed. She knew what he was thinking. She smiled again and waved her finger at him warningly at the verse:

I have heard the mermaids singing, each to each.
I do not think that they will sing to me.

Ramzy sat there thinking that she was not as simple a person as he had thought. She seemed closely attached to certain principles. He also sensed that she was full of guilt feelings.

Eliot finished reciting his poem. Ramzy waited for Pamela to say something, but she did not. There was an uncomfortable silence.

He asked her, "How do you feel now?"

"Not so bad."

Silence again.

"You don't regret having stayed?"

"Why should I regret it?"

"You could be exposing yourself to danger unnecessarily."

"You mean you think I'm out of my mind, right?"

"Maybe. I just mean that this place is dangerous."

Pamela said nothing further. Quiet. Total quiet. Ramzy was glad that she was there. The day before, at this same time, he was worrying about a raid on the airport. Now the possibility did not concern him at all.

He switched on the radio. Another patriotic military song. He did not turn it off, but listened. He looked at his watch. It was almost midnight.

Suddenly Pamela got up and said, "Will you excuse me? I have to go to bed now. I'm really very tired."

"Well, of course. Feel free."

Pamela went off to her bedroom. Ramzy turned to a foreign station and heard the newscaster say that on Monday morning Israeli aircraft had destroyed the greater part of the Egyptian air force after catching them by surprise, while the planes were still on the ground. For some reason Israel was refraining from confirming this news.

He switched to an Arab station, where there still was talk of an Arab counteroffensive. This news was followed by another patriotic song.

Ramzy went to bed, but he could not sleep.

The bride Palestine had been abducted by a hyena and taken to an inaccessible cave. The angry bridegroom had taken his gun, fired, but had missed the target. Then he had run and climbed a tree, which he named the Tree of Revolution in spite of its being so old. But the tree gave no protection. The hyena pissed on its tail and sprayed the bridegroom, casting a spell on him.

But Azmy Abdel Qadir had been wounded in the forehead. The blood had flowed. He was no longer under the spell. He would not climb the tree again. He would fight on, even if alone.

THE THIRD DAY

Death Is a Field

SHARP SCREAMS pierced everything in Jericho. Fire was devouring the soldiers. Gradually the screams diminished, turning into deep groans, then sighs, and finally nothing.

Taha Kanaan was still there fighting the fires. Planes continued to swoop over the houses, the streets, the army quarters, and the fields, shooting and dropping bombs and rockets. Terror throbbed in people's veins, and shivers bore into their bones.

The telephone rang in the town hall. No one answered. The telephone receptionist had fled. Taha, now in the air raid shelter with a number of other officials, listened as the phone rang. It went on and on, but no one moved. At last Taha ran out and climbed the stairs in the dark. He felt his way to the phone and lifted the receiver. An angry voice told him that the planes had blown up two army camps, which were burning fiercely.

The speaker's voice grew ever angrier as he demanded, "Where are the fire-fighters? No one is answering the phone."

Taha sped in the jeep to the fire station. He found some men and told them to follow him to one of the camps. They found the whole camp ablaze. Tongues of flame were turning the night into day. The firemen directed their hoses at the fire, but it only burned more fiercely. It seemed to flow along with the water, even darting out over its surface. They were amazed. They did not realize that the camp was alight with napalm. Everything, even the water, was burning. They felt helpless, but continued their resistance.

Some soldiers ran up to them, with flames coming from their bodies. They threw themselves in front of the hoses, but the flames continued to eat at their flesh. Their screams penetrated everything. No one knew what to do.

When morning came, Taha realized how hopeless it was. The Jordanian army passed through Jericho. News spread that the army was withdrawing to the bridge, and the people of Jericho and the refugee camps panicked. Everything was falling to pieces. There was nothing to hold things together. Feet raced in all directions. No one was in authority. No one had control over himself. Waves of refugees from Jerusalem, Hebron, Ramallah, and elsewhere surged through Jericho on their way to the bridge. Panic spread. Three large refugee camps in the region were emptied.

Taha did not run. He no longer had control over the

people, but he did not want to lose control over himself. He would never retreat, never leave his farm and his house. He had worked all his life to have his own farm, and he would not leave now, as he had in 1948. He did not want to become a refugee for the second time. This time it was impossible for him to start his life again.

But crowds of people were withdrawing. It seemed that everyone in Jericho was leaving. It was unbelievable. He would never understand the world. Taha longed to catch sight of an Israeli soldier so that he could tear him apart. But he had not seen even one. It was as though this were not a real war at all. The enemy consisted of planes, too many to count. If he could find just one Israeli soldier! Or even a detachment of them, for that matter. He would charge them and explode a grenade in their midst. He was not afraid to die—in fact, he longed to make an offering of his life, but he could not even do that. There was no way he could fight, no way for him to be brave. He could not die with honor. Taha felt he could scarcely go on living, with his head on his shoulders, his ribs encaging his body. All he could fight was his own shadow.

Taha stood directly in front of the refugees and threatened them, but they surged onward. He wished they would trample him down, but they merely skirted round him. He remained alive. Once more his country was breaking into pieces. And there was nothing he could do.

Hopelessly, he wandered off toward home. He could not find his family. They too had left. They probably were out in the fields. He thought about his wife, his daughters, and his son, Darwish. Perhaps something had happened to them. He began running like a child, searching frantically for them among the crowds. At last he found them. They all ran toward him when they spotted him, as if he were returning from the jaws of death.

He asked his wife, "Why did you leave the house?"

She made no reply, just shook her head.

His brother Issam suggested, "Let's cross the bridge before the planes start bombing us. The crowds are getting worse here, and the enemy is certain to spot us."

Taha objected, "No, no. We're not crossing the bridge. I don't want to be a refugee for the second time. No, no. Impossible."

"Personally," argued Issam, "I don't want to leave, but the whole family keep insisting."

There was a period of silence. His wife offered Taha a piece of bread. He brushed it aside, insisting he was not hungry.

"But you've not eaten for two days."

"I'm not hungry."

The planes were still flying overhead in endless formations, bombing relentlessly. They came down so low they seemed almost to touch the ground, in line like the teeth of a comb passing through hair. Air raid sirens sounded continuously. One of the planes dropped some leaflets saying, "Surrender and be safe!" and "The Israeli defense forces are stronger than all the Arab armies put together."

Taha ripped up the leaflet he had read. His wife came over to him and said, "What's the use? What are you trying to prove?"

"I'm not trying to prove anything. I just want to stay put, to stay here. Don't you understand?"

"You don't care about your family?"

"Yes, of course I do. Of course I care about my family. That's why I want to stay."

His eldest daughter, Adla, now joined in: "I'm with you, Father. I shall stay with you."